THE EX WHO
CONNED A PSYCHIC

Sally Berneathy

Chapter One

Amanda roared into the parking lot of the Dallas Police Department substation and brought her Harley Sportster to a stop. Charley was, of course, riding on the back. In the two years they'd been married he hadn't spent a lot of time hanging around, but now that he was dead, she couldn't get rid of him.

She locked the bike, dismounted, slid off her helmet, and glared at him. "Do not start on me again!"

Charley spread his hands in a gesture of innocence. The September sunlight glinted off his blond hair much as it had done in life, though everything about him, including his hair, was translucent in his ghostly state. "I just think that detective's taking up too much of your time, making you come back in for more questions again."

"Really? We're trying to make sure those three creeps who murdered Dawson's parents and kidnapped his brother are put away for the rest of their lives, and you think it's taking too much of my time?"

Charley shrugged and looked away. "Seems to me you could have done it over the phone instead of in person."

"You're jealous, aren't you? That's what this is all about. It's not about how much time it takes. It's just because you think I'm attracted to Jake Daggett." She was, but she wasn't going to admit it to Charley.

Charley's cheeks flushed faintly pink. Interesting that he could still blush when he had no blood and no body to hold any blood. He looked away and didn't respond to her accusation. Lying had been his favorite form of communication in life, but in death Charley couldn't lie so he sometimes had difficulty maintaining a conversation.

Amanda started across the parking lot toward the front door of the substation.

"You could at least wait until I'm dead," he mumbled.

"You are dead. If you hadn't been murdered, our divorce would have eventually become final no matter how long you fought it. Either way, I'm not married to you anymore and it's none of your business if I decide to date somebody."

While it wasn't any of his business, his presence was a definite deterrent to any sort of relationship. Bound to her by an invisible tether, he couldn't get farther away than a few hundred yards and usually refused to go even that far, especially when Detective Jake Daggett was around.

"You're a cold woman, Amanda."

"Actually, I'm a little hot after riding over here in this leather jacket. I think the temperature must be about ninety already."

"Amanda Caulfield?"

Amanda looked up at the sound of her name. A young woman with dark hair bounced down the steps leading to the front door of the station.

The woman paused in front of Amanda, her smile bright, her brown eyes sparkling. "Don't tell me you don't remember me. Teresa Landow. I sat behind you in third period history class."

Amanda forced her lips upward in what she hoped was a reasonable facsimile of a smile. "Teresa. Of course I remember you." Like she'd ever forget one of the most annoying people she'd ever met. Teresa—cheerleader, prom queen, homecoming queen, girl most likely to succeed and to be hated by every other girl in school. Amanda gave her a quick once over. Damn. She still looked great in her skin tight jeans and boots with three inch heels that elevated her tiny frame almost to Amanda's height. Her hair, falling sleek and straight down her back, glinted blue black in the sunlight.

"You're looking good," Teresa said. "Is that gear for real? Are you a biker chick now?"

"I ride motorcycles, yes." Amanda glanced over her shoulder. "That's one of mine."

Charley wrapped his arms around himself and gave a mock shiver. "From the frigid tone of your voice, I'm going to take a wild guess and say this woman was not your best friend."

Amanda turned back to Teresa who appeared to be looking at Charley. Of course she wasn't since nobody but Amanda had the privilege...or curse...of being able to see and hear Charley.

Teresa's gaze shifted to the Harley. "I've always thought riding a motorcycle would be fun."

"It is. I got my first bike the summer after we graduated. Oh, but you left just before graduation, didn't you?" Even as Amanda spoke, she remembered the stories and wished she could call back her words. She didn't like Teresa but hadn't meant to be cruel by bringing up painful memories.

Teresa shrugged. "Dad made some bad investments and we lost the house. Moved to a less expensive part of town." She recited the disastrous events as if they were of little importance though Amanda recalled she had been devastated at the time.

Charley edged closer. "Guess you got her put down for whatever she did to you in high school."

Amanda forced herself not to look at him, not to reprimand him, to keep her gaze focused on Teresa. "Well, it's great to see you again." She moved forward to go around the woman and continue into the substation.

But Teresa stepped backward, remaining in her path. "Your dad's a lawyer, isn't he?"

"He was. He's a judge now." The woman came out of the police station and asked about a lawyer. Amanda had a feeling she knew what was coming next.

Teresa's cheerleader smile drooped slightly. "Oh. Well, if he's a judge, I may be seeing him soon. My husband was murdered, and they're looking at me as a suspect just because I hated him and had good reason to kill him."

Amanda flinched and felt a flash of sympathy for the woman she'd envied and hated in high school. "Been there, done that."

"No kidding?" Teresa's gaze flickered to the side, again almost as if she could see Charley. "Your husband was murdered and they blamed you? Who'd you get to represent you in court?"

"It didn't go that far. They didn't have any evidence against me. It was all circumstantial, and we found the real killer."

"That's wonderful! Maybe you could help me find out who murdered my husband."

"Oh, well, uh…"

"She probably did it herself," Charley said.

"I did not!" Teresa snapped.

Charley moved closer to Amanda. "Okay, that was weird."

Teresa couldn't have heard him and responded to his accusation. Maybe she was responding to Amanda's hesitation, assuming it meant she thought Teresa was guilty. "I'm sure you didn't. The police will find the truth."

Teresa rolled her eyes. "Not likely. I just talked to them, and they don't want the truth. They only want a conviction. The cop in there was very rude to me, acted like he didn't believe a word I said. Told me not to leave town."

Amanda wasn't sure how many homicide detectives they had at the small substation, probably not a lot. "What was the detective's name?"

"Jake Daggett. Hot guy, but a complete jerk."

Charley snorted.

"That's the guy who had my case. He's okay. He just likes to come on as the bad cop. I'm not sure they have a good cop. You'll be fine." Again Amanda tried to move around Teresa.

Teresa took her arm to detain her. All traces of the happy cheerleader were gone. She looked downright desperate. "Amanda, I need your help."

"My help? I guess I could ask my dad to recommend a good criminal lawyer." She tried to free her arm but the smaller woman's grip was astonishingly strong.

"I'm a psychic," Teresa said.

"A what? Psychic? Like on television?"

"Yes, exactly like on television. My grandmother was too. I inherited it from her. My mother didn't have the gift or maybe we wouldn't have lost everything." She grinned wryly. "We're gypsies. Well, we were a few generations ago. I've always had the gift, and it's how I've been earning a living since Anthony and I split up."

"You were separated when he was murdered? Me too." Amanda felt a glimmer of kinship with this woman she didn't particularly like. "We were getting a divorce but he got himself killed before it was final." The archaic expression was the way she looked at it. Charley had got himself killed by being a greedy blackmailer.

Teresa stepped back and held a hand to her chest, her eyes wide. "Me too! He left me for some blond bimbo who had a bigger boob job than mine and then he got himself killed."

"Your husband cheated on you? So did mine!" They were practically sisters.

"We need to go somewhere and talk."

"I can't right now. I have to meet with Detective Daggett about another case. Maybe we can get together for lunch sometime." Even though they shared membership in the cheated-on sisterhood, Amanda wasn't sure she wanted to pursue any kind of involvement with the former cheerleader turned psychic.

"How about dinner tonight? We have way more to talk about than we can get to over just lunch."

"Well, uh…"

"Amanda, this is probably going to sound crazy, but I swear it's the truth. You have a spirit attached to you."

Amanda gasped.

Charley gasped. "She can see me?"

"Of course I can see you. You're a man, tall and blond with blue eyes and wearing a white knit shirt and khaki slacks."

She could see him. Somebody else could see Charley. Amanda bit her lip and tried to take it in. She had been certain she was the only one who could see and hear Charley. But now, unless this was some kind of a trick, Teresa could see him. "It's my ex-husband, Charley." Her voice came out barely above a whisper.

"Oh, you know he's here? I didn't realize you were psychic too."

Amanda shook her head. "I'm not. He's the only ghost I've ever seen. I hope he's the only one I ever have to see."

"Did he tell you who killed him? Is that the way you were able to prove your innocence?"

"Yes, I did," Charley said proudly. "You can really see me?"

"I couldn't miss you. You still have a strong presence on this plane. You didn't get very far away. But I can't see my own husband's spirit, and none of the spirits I've talked to have seen him either. That's got to be why I've been led to you, Amanda. I don't know if he's hiding from me because he wants to see me go to prison or he's just on such a low plane, the other spirits can't see him. But maybe, since your husband's spirit is so close to the earthly plane, he can talk to mine and find out who murdered him."

"Uh…" It was the only thing Amanda could think of to say.

"I don't know your husband," Charley protested. "How am I supposed to talk to him?"

"You haven't been doing this very long, have you?" Teresa asked. "You're stuck at a very low level. You must have been a bad husband."

"I..." Charley stopped with his mouth open. His lips twisted and he tried again to form words, probably to deny he was a bad husband. "I..." He sighed and gave up the attempt. "I was a bad husband."

Amanda laughed. "He can't lie anymore. It's a terrible state for somebody who couldn't tell the truth before."

Teresa compressed her lips and nodded. "He's definitely at a really low level. But if you help me, I'll help him move on to a higher plane."

"You will?" The feeling of sisterhood was growing. "You can help him move on?"

"Of course. I can help him move into the light." She shrugged. "I'm a medium. I call myself a psychic because the term is more marketable, but actually I'm a medium. I talk to dead people."

Whatever she called herself, she'd just become Amanda's new best friend.

Chapter Two

After making plans to meet Teresa for dinner, Amanda and Charley continued into the police station.

"She makes me feel almost real again because she can see me," he said as they climbed the steps. "Of course you're the most important person in my life and having you see me is what matters, but how would you feel if most people just looked right through you like you didn't even exist?"

Amanda was also thrilled that Teresa could see Charley but for a very different reason. Teresa had said she could help him move on, into the light. Divorces often took a long time, and the year since Amanda had filed for divorce from Charley wasn't an unusually long period compared to some. Nevertheless, most people going through a divorce didn't stay within a couple of hundred feet of each other twenty-four/seven.

She stopped at the front desk where a young woman sat behind a bullet-proof partition. "Amanda Caulfield to see Detective Jake Daggett."

The receptionist smiled. "I'll let him know you're here."

"She smiled at me," Charley said. "Maybe she can see me too."

"Thank you." Amanda felt certain the woman could not see him, but she could be wrong. She'd been certain Teresa couldn't see him.

"I'm getting stronger. Pretty soon I may get my body back." He waved at the young woman. "Hi! I'm Charley!"

Without a glance in Charley's direction, the receptionist dialed an extension.

He sighed. "Maybe not everybody can see me just yet."

Maybe just Teresa. Maybe she really was a psychic or a medium or a psychic medium. Amanda didn't believe in psychics and mediums, but a few months ago, she hadn't believed in ghosts.

A door opened behind her, and Amanda turned to see Jake. His dark hair looked as if he'd been running his hands through it all morning. He probably had. His brown eyes gave him a dangerous look and Amanda knew from experience how intimidating he could be. But at the moment sparks glowed from the depths of those eyes, and his lips curved upward in a smile. She found her own lips responding.

"Hi," she said.

"Hi. Glad you could come by."

"No problem. Glad to help."

Charley darted between them and scowled. "Why don't you two just get a room?"

"Let's find a conference room where we can go over these documents." Jake lifted the folder he held in one hand.

Amanda winced at his unconscious response to Charley's snipe. She stepped around Charley to walk through the door Jake held open. Charley reached out as if to stop her. A chill shivered through her as she moved determinedly through his arm.

When she brushed past Jake, even though they didn't touch, she felt the warmth of his body. A nice contrast to Charley's chilliness.

"Right over there." Jake pointed with the folder.

Amanda had first been to the station a few months ago as a suspect in Charley's murder. Though her last couple of visits had involved meeting with Jake to give her statement on the recent kidnapping and murders—a much more positive experience than the first visit—she did not like being in the dismal interrogation rooms. They were all the same...rectangular with ugly rectangular furniture, and they were all creepy. Maybe the ghosts of the guilty people who'd been grilled in those rooms lingered just out of sight. She'd have to ask Teresa if she'd seen any.

She preceded Jake into the room, set helmet, gloves and keys on the ugly rectangular table, and sat tentatively on one of the ugly wooden chairs. Charley sat beside her. He didn't pull out the chair, of course, just sank through the table.

Jake took a seat across from her and spread the contents of his file on the table. "If you could look over these, and if everything's correct, sign above your name, then I'll witness your signature." He slid a couple of the documents toward her.

Amanda scanned them, verified that everything was true to the best of her knowledge, and signed.

Jake scrawled his signature below hers then put the papers back into his folder.

Their meeting was over. A few minutes, a couple of pen strokes. Wasn't that what he'd said when he called? But she felt irrationally disappointed. She wasn't sure exactly what she'd thought might happen in the police substation, but this brief encounter wasn't it.

She rose from her chair, but Jake didn't move. He studied her, his gaze intense, no longer sparkling. He cleared his throat. If it had been anybody other than the self-possessed cop, she'd have sworn Jake looked uncomfortable. That wasn't possible, of course. Maybe he had gas.

"So how are Dawson and his brother doing?" he asked. "Any problems with PTSD?"

Amanda sat down again. "No. They're fine. Actually, they seem more relaxed than before. I think being able to come out of hiding and not have to tell lies about who they are has been an enormous relief."

Jake nodded. "Good." He clicked the end of his pen a couple of times. "And your mother? Is she doing okay?"

"Which one?"

Jake grinned, his features relaxing a little. She'd been right. He was uncomfortable. What was up with that? Was he going to tell her something she didn't want to hear? Question her about…what? She hadn't done anything illegal lately. "Both of them," he said. "The redhead with the gun and the socialite with the Mercedes."

Amanda laughed.

Charley snorted. "Oh, please. I think I'm gonna be sick. I wonder what ghost vomit looks like."

13

"Both my mothers are fine," she said.

Jake slid the pen through his fingers, tapping first the top, then the bottom on the table. "You're going to be around to testify at the trial, right?"

"Of course." They'd already discussed that. She was eager to testify, to send the evil trio to prison. What was he working up to?

"You're not concerned about those crazy people retaliating?"

She laughed again. That was it? He was worried about her being afraid to testify? "I sleep with a .38 in my nightstand. Besides, if I testify against them, they'll be in prison for the rest of their lives. That will make it pretty hard for them to retaliate."

"Or they may be dead. Their crimes make them eligible for the death penalty. Does that bother you?"

"Seriously? After what those people did, you think I wouldn't want them eliminated from this world? Is that what this is all about? You're worried I won't show up for the trial because I couldn't stand it if those awful people got the death penalty and my testimony was part of the reason?"

He dropped the pen to the table top and leaned forward intently. "No. That's not what this is about. Even if you decided not to testify, we've got plenty on them with Dawson and Grant. This is..." He swallowed and leaned back then cleared his throat and tried again. "This is about me asking you to go out with me, and for some reason, I'm having a really hard time doing that."

Amanda blinked. "Oh!"

Charley rolled his eyes. "Oh, good grief."

Jake grimaced and stood, focusing his attention on the folder. "I'm sorry. Forget it. I'm being inappropriate."

"Yes! I mean, no, you're not. Yes, I'd love to go out with you."

Charley groaned.

Jake sat back down and smiled. "How about Saturday night? We could go to dinner and catch a movie. Is that what people still do on dates?"

"Works for me. I haven't done this in a while, and it sounds like maybe you haven't either."

He shrugged and rifled the papers in the file with his thumb. "Yeah, you're not the only one with a crazy ex."

Charley frowned. "What does that mean? What's he trying to say?"

Jake's meaning was clear. If Charley didn't understand, it was because he didn't want to.

Amanda wasn't sure how she was going to manage a date with both Jake and Charley in attendance, but she wasn't going to refuse. One way or the other, death or divorce, she was not married to Charley. Maybe her new friend Teresa would be able to move him to a higher plane soon. That brought back her thoughts of Teresa's crime.

"Oh, hey, on my way in here I ran into somebody I went to high school with, somebody you just talked to. Teresa Landow."

Jake shook his head. "Teresa Landow? Oh, you mean Teresa Hocker?"

"Hocker? Yeah, she said she was married. Well, that she was a widow. That you think she killed her husband."

Jake arched a dark eyebrow and said nothing.

"Come on! I'm going to see this all on the ten o'clock news. Not to mention I'm having dinner with the woman tonight. I'd kind of like to know if I'm going to be breaking bread with a murderer." Not that it made any real difference. Even if Teresa was a murderer, some husbands deserved to be murdered, and she needed Teresa's help getting rid of Charley.

"At this point, she's a person of interest. We found the body yesterday so we haven't had time to go through all the evidence."

"So it's the old *the estranged wife is the first suspect.*"

Jake grinned, one side of his lips quirking slightly higher than the other, giving him a mischievous rather than dangerous appearance. "It does happen that way sometimes. Estranged wives can be really angry. They've been known to make threats."

"You mean things like stripping the husband in question naked, tying his hands and feet, pouring honey on him and leaving him on a hill of fire ants in west Texas in the middle of August? Drilling a hole through his forehead, inserting a peg and hanging a potted plant from it? Those are just pleasant fantasies that help a woman get through an ugly divorce." She folded her hands on the table. "So, was Teresa's divorce ugly?"

Jake laughed. "You don't want to know whether she's a murderer. You just want to hear the gossip about her."

Amanda shrugged. "Gossip, murder, whatever. I need to be prepared. How did the husband die? Should I worry about her bringing a gun to the restaurant or using the steak knife to slit my throat? In that case, I suppose we should just order cheese enchiladas."

"You have a talent for melodrama."

"Thank you. Now, how did she off the evil ex? Anthony, I think she called him."

"Anthony Hocker, owner of Anthony Hocker and Sons Investments."

"Sons? They have kids?" Teresa didn't seem the motherly type.

"No kids. Some people do that with company names because they think it makes them sound more trustworthy. Anyway, if you'd actually been watching the ten o'clock news, you'd already know about the murder. It was the top story on all the channels. Somebody shot him three times in the face in his own garage, poured gasoline all over him and set him on fire. Between the gun shots and the fire, his body was so badly damaged we were only able to identify him from his wallet, his watch and ring, and the fact that he was the only person in his home."

Amanda drew in a deep breath and sat back in her chair. "Wow. That does sound like the murder was personal."

Charley shuddered. "Maybe it's not such a good thing that woman can see me."

All of a sudden Teresa had become *that woman*?

"And, yes, their divorce was ugly and high profile," Jake said. "He had a lot of money and a young girlfriend. He had enough money to pay for a shark attorney to try to keep his wife from getting anything. Their divorce has made the news a couple of times. The wife has quite a temper. She threatened him on the ten o'clock news. That's pretty damning."

Amanda flinched. At least her threats to Charley never made the news, but plenty of neighbors had heard, giving rise to suspicions about her when Charley was murdered. "That doesn't make her all bad just because she was married to some jerk who knew how to push her buttons." But it might be a good idea to get Teresa's help in sending Charley on his way as soon as possible before Amanda had to visit her in prison. It could be difficult to process a spirit in the middle of the prison visitation room.

Jake folded his hands. "As I said, at this point, she's a person of interest. So are several other people."

"Is she the most interesting of those several people?"

"We'll know more when Ross finishes his work on the trace evidence."

"Ross Minatelli? The forensics guy who worked on Dawson's case?"

"Yeah, there's only one Ross Minatelli."

"Oh, good. I liked him. Is he around? Could I maybe talk to him?"

"Yes, he's around, and, no, you can't talk to him. Go meet your friend for dinner and have a good time. Just be sure to take your .38."

Amanda sucked in a quick breath at his implied warning. Did Jake have evidence he wasn't telling her about? "Really?"

"I'm kidding. Relax. Even if she killed her husband, she has no reason to kill you."

"That's true. I hated her in high school, but she didn't even know I existed. I was surprised she remembered me." Amanda rose and gathered up her things from the table. "Okay, so I'll…" She swallowed, suddenly feeling like the awkward nerd she'd been back in high school when Teresa was the cheerleader and she was the invisible girl.

I'll see you on Saturday. The words stuck in her throat.

"Saturday night," he said. "Pick you up about six? Is that too early?"

"Six is good."

Jake escorted her to the front door. "I'll check movie times and call you."

Amanda stepped out into the warm September sunshine. She felt herself smiling as she walked down the steps toward the parking lot.

"You are not seriously going on a date with that man. You're a married woman!"

That wiped the smile from her face. She whirled on Charley. "Death parted us, damn it! When we were married, you were never around. You were always off somewhere with some woman or working some scam. If you're going to insist we're still married, then you need to stay away all the time like you did before."

"I'm not going anywhere. If you try to go on a date with that man, I'll be right there, reminding you that you're not free to do that."

Amanda brushed past him and continued toward her motorcycle. Teresa had no idea what she was getting into, wanting to establish contact with her deceased estranged husband. She was worried she might go to prison if he didn't tell her who murdered him. Going to prison or being haunted by her ex…it was a toss-up.

Chapter Three

Amanda pulled into the parking lot of Amanda's Motorcycles and More. Located in the northwest section of Dallas off Harry Hines Boulevard, it wasn't the best area of town but it wasn't the worst either. A few older homes mingled with small businesses like hers, and she was able to have her shop on the first floor with her apartment above it. Convenient.

She entered the shop to find her assistant, Dawson, sitting on the floor beside a new, shiny black Indian Chief Vintage bike. "Guy just brought it in this morning," he said without looking up from the design he was creating. His attention was completely focused on what he was doing. Motorcycle art and computers were his passions. Amanda wasn't sure which he was most passionate about.

"Nice," she said. "Both the bike and your art work. When you get a chance, I have some things I need you to look up on the Internet for me."

"Okay."

Charley laughed. "Hope you're not in a hurry. He's not going to look up from that bike for a while. It is pretty. I'm glad they're making Indian bikes again. I used to have an old Indian. Wish I still had that bike. Wish I could still ride motorcycles."

"You ride on the back of mine everywhere I go," she muttered.

"It's not the same thing."

Amanda ignored his wistful tone and started toward the room designated an office because it housed the computer and landline telephone, and it had a door that would close.

"Some guy's waiting for you," Dawson said. "I put him in the corner room since there's nothing in there but some greasy parts. I gave him a folding chair."

Amanda stopped and looked down at her assistant, at the back of his head because he was still totally focused on his work. "What guy?"

"I don't know. Somebody who knew Charley. I told him I could have you call him, but he wanted to wait. He's been there about an hour."

Amanda peered at the opening of the enclosure in question but couldn't see anything except various used parts lying on the floor.

Charley disappeared into the room then came out again, noticeably paler. "Don't go in there!"

What horror could make a ghost go pale? Amanda's heart constricted and she suddenly wished her .38 was closer than the nightstand upstairs. She scanned the motorcycle parts and tools scattered around the area. Maybe she should take a large wrench to meet this guy.

"Let's go get an early lunch." Charley tried to take her arm. His touch sent an icy shiver through her.

She stepped away from him, suddenly more suspicious of him than frightened of whoever sat waiting. "Why?"

Dawson looked up from his work and pushed his glasses higher on his nose. "I don't know why. He just said he wanted to wait so I let him. Is there a problem? Do you want me to go with you to talk to him?"

"No!" Charley protested. "Don't drag Dawson into this. Let's go for a bike ride. I really miss riding a motorcycle." His flustered attempts to keep her from meeting with the mysterious man in her office actually calmed Amanda. If Charley was worried about her safety, he'd tell her outright. His nervousness told her he was worried about what the mysterious man was going to tell her. It wasn't the first time that had happened both in life and after death. It usually involved either a woman he'd cheated with or somebody he'd scammed.

"I'll be fine," she told Dawson. "But keep an eye on the doorway in case I need you."

He nodded, already immersed in his work again. She headed toward the small room.

"Amanda, you don't want to do this. No good can come of talking to Ronald Collins. He's a complete jerk. Gambler. Drug dealer. Crazy man. Sorry excuse for a human being."

"Friend of yours?" she asked.

"No!"

Amanda entered the room. Sitting on a metal folding chair among the dirty, greasy motorcycle parts was a dirty, greasy man. He wasn't really dirty or greasy, but he somehow gave off that aura, especially his eyes which were bottomless pits of grease and dirt.

Even though he didn't bother to get up when she entered the room—an inexcusable error of etiquette in Texas—Amanda could tell he was tall. Arms with stringy muscles protruded from his wife-beater T-shirt, and his gut strained against the thin fabric. His scraggly brown beard seemed an attempt to make up for the total lack of hair on his shiny head.

"Can I help you?" she asked, remaining in the open doorway in case she needed to back out fast.

The facial hair moved as if it was alive...or had small creatures running around in its depths. The man was smiling, though his cold eyes weren't. "You're Amanda. Charley showed me pictures of you. I'm Ronald Collins. Me and your husband used to be friends."

"I doubt it."

The facial hair did another dance, moving in a downward pattern. Frowning? Scowling? Glaring? Threatening? His eyes remained flat, dead and greasy. "What's that supposed to mean?"

She crossed her arms and tried to match the coldness in his gaze. "Charley didn't have friends. He had enemies and criminal associates and scam targets. Which one were you?"

Ronald Collins nodded. "Yeah, that's Charley. Well." He rose, and Amanda felt a brief flash of hope that he was leaving, giving up on whatever mission had led him to her place. Instead he pulled a piece of paper from the back pocket of his stained khakis. Slowly he unfolded it and offered it to her.

Accustomed to working on motorcycles, Amanda had no problem with getting her hands dirty, but she flinched from touching that sheet of paper that had been in the man's back pocket, was probably warm with the heat from his body.

"What is it?" She tucked her hands safely behind her. "If that's some kind of an IOU, you need to file a claim against Charley's estate. He's dead, and he was in debt when he died so I wouldn't count on recovering much."

"And he was married to you when he died. Last I heard, Texas is still a community property state. I had to pay off enough bills for my ex-old-ladies to know that."

If only Charley had signed those divorce papers before he died. Amanda was pretty sure there was no such thing as a posthumous divorce, but she could ask Dawson to look on the Internet just in case.

Collins thrust the paper toward her and Amanda stepped backward.

"Think you're too good to touch something I been handling? Think my hands are too dirty?"

Amanda flinched as the man correctly expressed her feelings, though those feelings had more to do with the ugly expression in his eyes than the dirt under his fingernails.

Collins chuckled, turned and laid the paper on the seat of the chair where he'd been sitting. "Take a look at it when I'm gone. Take it to your daddy, the highfalutin judge Charley had in his pocket, and let him look it over. I talked to a lawyer. It's all legal." The facial hairs moved up and around. This time a smile settled in his eyes, but it was the kind of smile the executioner gave just before he dropped the guillotine. "This is a copy. I still have the original Charley signed selling this place to me."

Anger swelled inside Amanda, clenching her jaw and knotting her stomach. She did not doubt for one minute that Charley had signed over her shop to this obnoxious man.

Collins swaggered toward the doorway, toward Amanda. He disgusted her. He frightened her. But she stood her ground, meeting him glare for glare, refusing to let him leave with the idea that he'd beaten her. "Get off my property." She moved aside to let him pass.

Again he gave her the executioner's smile. "*Whose* property?"

She turned to watch the man walk out of the shop as fury seethed through every inch of her body. He paused a couple of times along the way to run his fingers possessively over bikes waiting to be repaired. Amanda gritted her teeth and said nothing until the front door closed behind him.

She snatched the paper off the chair and looked at it. A handwritten—Charley's handwriting—transfer of *the building and all contents*...signed by Charley and two witnesses. "CHARLEY!"

Dawson shot up, paint brush in one hand, eyes wide. "What? What's happened?"

He'd been completely engrossed in his work, totally unaware of the drama playing out nearby. Typical Dawson.

"That man who just left, the one waiting for me. He's got some kind of document saying Charley signed over this shop to him."

Dawson frowned. "I don't understand. This is your place. Charley never worked here."

"I know. But unfortunately, I was married to the jerk when I bought this place and I was still married to him when he signed it over to that creep. I doubt if he can enforce the terms of that document, but I think he's going to try to cause me some problems."

"Charley's been dead for almost four months. When did he sign it?"

"Over a year ago, and that brings up a good question. Why did that man suddenly decide to do this? As soon as you have time, could you get on the Internet and see what you can find out about him?"

"Give me ten more minutes. I'm almost finished with the first phase of this design."

"I'll put this on the desk beside the computer." She waved the sweaty, crumpled paper through the air as if to blow off some of the contamination. "I need to know what you can find on Ronald Wayne Collins."

Dawson sat down and resumed work on the Indian.

"Oh, and also Teresa Landow. Teresa Landow Hocker."

Dawson looked up at her. "The woman accused of killing her husband?"

"That's the one. I went to high school with her. Ran into her today and we're meeting for dinner. Jake wouldn't tell me anything about the evidence against her, so I'm counting on you."

"Oh!" Dawson blinked and, with the back of the hand holding the paint brush, shoved his glasses higher on his nose. "You're worried your friend might be guilty? Well, you were suspected of murdering Charley, and you were innocent."

Since Amanda had fantasized about Charley's murder several times, she wasn't sure if she could be classified as *innocent*. Not guilty of murder, but not quite *innocent*. "Right," she said. "I didn't kill him. And Teresa said she didn't kill her husband. She's probably telling the truth, but I'd just like to know a little more about her and what the cops have on her and all that sort of thing before we get together tonight." *So I'll know if we can take our time getting Charley on his way out of here or if we need to hurry before they lock her up.*

"Will do." Dawson returned to his painting.

Amanda went to the small office and laid the hand-written document on top of the papers already lying on the scarred wooden desk. She needed to catch up on filing, put the orders, receipts and other business papers in alphabetical order in the metal filing cabinet, move anything important to their small safe.

But not today.

"Charley," she said quietly. "I know you're here. You're always here. You might as well talk to me."

He appeared at the other end of the desk as if putting a safe distance between them, as if he thought she could physically hurt him for his misdeeds.

If only!

"It was a friendly poker game."

She arched an eyebrow. "Friendly?"

"Okay, it was a cutthroat game of poker. Four of us. I was losing, but I knew my luck was just about to turn. You know how you get that feeling sometimes?"

Amanda stared at him wordlessly.

"Okay, maybe you don't. But I *knew* I was going to start winning. It was one of those psychic things, like Teresa gets." He shifted from one foot to the other though neither of those feet touched the floor. "I guess you had to be there. But I knew if I just had enough money for another hand, I'd win back everything I'd lost."

"I don't even want to know how much that would be."

"Good choice. No point in dwelling on the past." He waved a hand through the air. "The past is over and done. Let it go. We have to move on."

Amanda spread her arms in frustration. "Not when the past comes up to bite me! So you signed over my shop...*my* shop...to that jerk for more gambling money?"

"Well, yeah, I guess you could put it that way."

"Is there another way you'd put it?"

"I wrote out that paper and he gave me two hundred dollars."

Amanda groaned. "*Two hundred dollars*? You sold my shop for two hundred dollars and then you gambled away that money?"

"No! I didn't sell this place. I just borrowed against it, and then I won. I paid him back."

"Really? You paid him back? Then what was all that about? Why is he trying to say he owns my shop? Why don't you tell me where you put the receipt, I'll show it to him, and this will all be over." There was, of course, no receipt. Charley would never have been that methodical.

He winced. "Well, I didn't exactly get a receipt. I mean, it was just between friends. And he said he tore up that thing I wrote."

"Oh, well, if he said he tore it up, then of course you had to believe him." She leaned toward him. "But he didn't tear it up, did he?"

"He tore up something. I was pretty excited about winning. Remember that time I came home with roses and took you out to eat at Rosewood Mansion the next evening? We had a great time, didn't we? That chocolate dessert you had looked really good."

Amanda ignored Charley's attempt to divert her attention. "Oh, Charley, you'd think the way you scammed everybody, you'd be more suspicious of other people."

He shrugged and looked at the floor. "Ronnie always had great weed. I might have been a little out of it that night."

Amanda straightened. "If you were under the influence of drugs, then you couldn't enter into a legal agreement." She slumped. "But how do we prove it? Not like anybody's going to take your word for it."

"Maybe. Remember, Teresa can see me too."

"Yeah, the testimony of a local psychic who's accused of killing her husband will probably carry a lot of weight."

"Are you talking to me?" Dawson came in and sat down in front of the computer.

"No," Amanda said. "Just…talking. I'll leave you alone while you work in case you want to hack into databases you don't want me to know about."

Dawson didn't comment. He was already immersed in the cyber world.

Amanda paused in the doorway. "Dawson, do you believe in ghosts?"

"Of course. I wouldn't want to be without it." He hit a few keys then moved the mouse around.

Of course? That wasn't what she'd expected. Computer geek, data-oriented Dawson wouldn't want to be without ghosts?

But he'd said *it* not *them*.

"It? Are you talking about some ghost in particular?" Had he been able to see Charley all this time but never admitted it because he didn't want to sound crazy?

He looked at her, his eyes large and guileless behind the thick lenses of his glasses. "I use Acronis, but there are several software programs out there."

"Acronis? Software? What?"

Dawson frowned. "Isn't that what you asked me about, ghosting the hard drive?"

"Uh…"

"Making a copy so if anything happens, the system crashes or something, I'll have a complete backup?"

"Not exactly. I was thinking more of the spirit kind of ghost."

Dawson nodded. "Oh, that kind of ghost. The concept isn't as strange as it sounds. Physics teaches us that nothing disappears, it just changes form. Some people believe our spirits simply vibrate at a frequency we can't see."

"I'm not vibrating," Charley said. "I'm standing perfectly still."

"So...you do believe in ghosts?" Amanda asked.

He shrugged. "String theory, black holes, infinity...there are a lot of concepts that most of us will never understand. Ghosts may be one of them."

That was certainly more open-minded than she'd expected Dawson to be. "Okay, well, just so you know, Teresa Landow, my former classmate, claims to be able to see the spirits of dead people."

"I see." Dawson turned his attention back to the computer screen. "It's certainly possible, but I've never seen any evidence that my parents are still around."

Too late Amanda realized how cruel her questions might be. His parents had been brutally murdered two years before, leaving Dawson alone to raise his young brother. She cleared her throat and tried to think of something to say that would be consoling. "Just because you can't see them doesn't mean they're not around." *You can't see Charley, but he's definitely here.* Maybe someday she'd tell Dawson about Charley. It might make him feel better about losing his parents.

She went back into the shop area and took out her cell phone. With a judge for her father and a lawyer for her birth mother, surely she could get some legal advice about the stupid paper Charley had signed.

Her dad was doubtless presiding in court at the moment, but she could call his clerk and leave a message. She didn't really want her mother...the mother who raised her...to hear about this latest problem. It would upset her. But so long as she called her dad at work, it would be okay.

Or she could call her birth mother, Sunny, who might or might not be available at the moment but always called her back as soon as she could.

She decided to call them both. Wouldn't want either of them to feel left out of the latest development in Charley's legacy.

Neither was available, so she left messages then set to work changing out a flywheel on a Honda. The job was simple, clear-cut, fulfilling. A wrench, a puller, everything cut and dried, solid metal. No ghosts, no questions of someone's guilt or innocence. If only she could spend all her time with motorcycles and ignore the complexities of human beings. And the ghosts of those human beings.

She finished the job and went back to the office where Dawson still sat in front of the computer.

"Find anything?" she asked.

"Actually, with those two people on the Internet, I'm surprised there's room out there for all that adware."

It was Dawson's attempt to make a joke. "Does that mean you found a lot?"

He nodded. "Ronald Collins has been married five times and divorced four. He's still married to number two, so I guess that makes him a bigamist during marriages three, four, and five."

Amanda frowned. "Really? Five women married that jerk? I'm going to assume he drugged them or held a gun to their heads. Any kids? Please tell me he has not passed his DNA along to innocent children."

"Three boys and one girl. Doesn't look like he's paying child support for any of them. He only works intermittently. His most recent job was laying carpet. He lost that over a year ago."

"Why?"

"There's no official reason given. Employers have to be very careful about listing reasons for letting employees go because they've been sued in the past. We live in a very litigious society. But some things this guy's done should wave a red flag to any future employer. He's been in trouble for just about any crime you can name. Failure to register a motor vehicle, possession of drug paraphernalia, failure to pay child support, possession of a controlled substance, possession of a controlled substance with intent to sell, gambling, drunk and disorderly, driving under the influence, spousal abuse…" He sighed and looked up at her. "Maybe it would be easier to tell you what he hasn't been accused of."

"Okay. What hasn't he been accused of?"

"Kidnapping and arson."

She gulped. "What about murder?"

"They charged him with murder in a bar fight a few years ago, but he got off on self-defense. This guy must have some really big legal fees."

"Nah," Charley said. "He trades drugs for services with a couple of lawyers."

"What a nice man Charley gave my shop to."

Charley lifted his arms and spread his hands. "I didn't give your shop away. I borrowed against it and paid him back."

"Did you find an address for him?" she asked Dawson.

"Several. Some of them aren't legitimate, some don't exist, some belong to large estates. Maybe he worked at those places at one time or another and used their addresses."

"Or maybe he burgled them and stole their addresses along with their valuables."

"Possible. In any event, I don't think we need to bother with most of his purported addresses. I've discounted those and the ones older than three years. The address on his driver's license which expired two years ago is an apartment a couple of miles from where I live. That's a possibility, though the place is supposedly rented to an elderly lady now. The most recent is one he gave the post office for forwarding his mail a few months ago. It's a house across town rented by a woman with three children. Property value indicates the house itself is virtually worthless, a tear down."

Amanda released a huge sigh as she perched on the side of the desk. "Great. He needs a job and a place to live. He's planning to live in my apartment and repair motorcycles in my shop."

Dawson shook his head. "I can't see any evidence he's ever owned a motorcycle or had a license to ride one. Of course, someone like him doesn't have a large personal presence on social media. He could be stealing and riding motorcycles every day without anything showing up."

"Nah," Charley said. "Ronnie's scared of motorcycles. He thinks people who ride them are crazy. More likely he wants your shop so he can cook up a little meth. He tried that one time in his apartment, but the neighbors noticed the smell. This place would be perfect with all the room and the outside lot separating you from your neighbors."

Amanda's jaw dropped. "Meth? He's planning to make meth in *my* shop?"

Dawson blinked rapidly a couple of times. "What? Meth? Amanda, what are you talking about? I never said the guy was making methamphetamine."

"Uh…but you didn't say he wasn't. It's just a, uh, sort of feeling I had. It probably doesn't matter. I don't think that man can do anything with that silly piece of paper. I called Sunny and Dad and left messages. I'll get their opinions, but surely that creep won't be able to do anything legally."

"And we won't let him bully you into anything," Charley said. "He does that a lot. Bullies people. Cheats at cards too, but he's not very good at it. I was better."

Amanda drew in a deep breath and closed her eyes. Charley's pride over being an expert in cheating at cards didn't bode well for his making it into the light.

"You also wanted to know about your classmate?" Dawson asked.

"Yes," Amanda said. She'd been so caught up in the horror that was Ronald Collins, she'd forgotten about Teresa. "Tell me about her." Though the question of whether Teresa had murdered her husband suddenly seemed inconsequential in the face of losing her shop or maybe her life to the scumbag Ronald Collins.

"Teresa Landow married Anthony Hocker five years ago. He was already wealthy and became wealthier. He made money and both of them spent it lavishly for a while. Then about six months ago he filed for divorce. She counter-filed, charging him with adultery. She was trying to get the terms of her pre-nup mitigated with the adultery charge."

"She signed a pre-nup?"

"A very stringent one. Not that it matters. Even if she got it set aside, Hocker no longer had a lot of assets so she wasn't going to get much from the divorce. But two months before he filed, she took out a million dollar life insurance policy on him. Of course, if she killed him, she can't benefit from her crime and she'll go to prison so that won't matter either."

"I hope she didn't, but it doesn't look good, does it? I mean, the pre-nup, the big insurance policy, and she said there was a new girlfriend."

"Yes, a twenty year old blonde who worked for him, Brianna Patterson. Teresa showed up at his office one day and caught the two of them together. Your friend went a little wild. Hit the girl with her purse and called her some rude names. The security guard had to drag her out of the building."

"Teresa has a temper. I remember in high school when she found out one of the other cheerleaders was dating her boyfriend, the football captain." Amanda smiled. "She put itching powder in her rival's pom-poms and her ex-boyfriend's helmet. During the next game, the two of them spent a lot of time scratching instead of playing and cheering."

"She got both of them? I hope nothing happens to the husband's new girlfriend. The deceased husband's new girlfriend."

"There's a lot of difference between itching powder and murder." But Teresa had hit the new girlfriend with her purse. That was up close, personal and physical. Not that Amanda really blamed her, considering the circumstances. She herself had never thought about attacking any of Charley's women, but she had thought about doing bodily harm to him. "How about news videos? Jake mentioned that she threatened him on the ten o'clock news. I never watch. It's too depressing."

Dawson nodded. "When they were coming out of the courthouse after the first hearing on the divorce, a couple of reporters were waiting. Caught her just as she came out the door, yelling that she'd take a gun and blow his brains out if he had any."

"Okay, that's not good, but a threat is a long way from the deed itself. Look how many times I threatened Charley."

Charley made a face. "Yeah, I remember all those times."

"Of course, if I'd had a million dollar life insurance policy on Charley, that would have gone a long way toward closing the distance between fantasizing and actually murdering him."

Chapter Four

Amanda arrived at the Mexican restaurant a few minutes late but still before Teresa. She requested a table on the patio outside where people would be less likely to notice the two of them talking to Charley.

As soon as she was seated in the shade of a large umbrella, she ordered a frozen margarita. She would probably need a couple of them. Not only did she have to worry that Teresa would be arrested before she could send Charley on his way, but both Sunny and her father had returned her calls and told her that Ronald Collins could cause her some problems with his nasty piece of paper. Neither thought his claim would prevail, but he could probably get some sleazy lawyer to take on the case and force her to fight him. The lawyers he paid with drugs qualified as *sleazy*.

Charley sat in the chair beside her. "Seems kinda strange that you can see me but Teresa can't see her husband, and she's a psychic. Maybe there's some kind of a rule that you can't talk to somebody after you kill them."

Amanda had given a passing thought to the same thing, but she wasn't about to agree with Charley. The waiter brought her drink along with a basket of chips and a bowl of hot sauce. She lowered her mouth to the straw of her drink and hoped none of the people seated at the tables around her would notice she was talking to her margarita. "I find it hard to believe she'd be asking you to talk to her dead husband if she murdered him. That could be kind of embarrassing if he ratted her out."

"I hope she didn't kill him. I like her."

"You like her because she can see you. And, of course, because she's an attractive woman. She could be holding a bloody knife and standing over a body, and you'd still like her because she's pretty."

"Teresa has a good soul. I can read people better now than I could before."

"Really? Just a few weeks ago you thought Nick Farner was a murderer, yet you failed to recognize Scott Warner as the psycho who killed Dawson's parents."

Charley rose and Amanda thought at first he was going to walk away in an effort to avoid her accusation. "There's Teresa."

Amanda turned to see her former classmate strolling toward them. She wore a white silk blouse, tight jeans with rhinestones down both legs, cowboy boots and a big smile. Several heads turned as she walked by and not just because she was pretty. Teresa had a self-confident air that attracted attention and envy.

"Hi, Amanda, Charley." She settled into the chair opposite Amanda, and Charley resumed his seat.

Amanda felt distinctly frumpy in her faded jeans, cotton blouse and motorcycle boots.

"I need one of those." Teresa focused her smile on the waiter who had followed her in and pointed to

Amanda's margarita. "If you get it here in the next five minutes, you'll save my life."

He returned her smile. "I'll do my best."

High school all over again, Amanda thought, then berated herself for being childish. It wasn't Teresa's fault she was beautiful and charming and self-confident. She couldn't blame the woman for utilizing those assets.

The waiter left and Teresa picked up the menu. "I recommend the fajitas. They're wonderful."

"I used to like fajitas," Charley said wistfully. "Could you maybe have them bring an extra plate for me so I can pretend I'm joining you all for dinner?"

"Of course we can." Teresa dipped a chip into the hot sauce.

"We can?" Amanda scanned the people sitting at tables near them. "Won't that look a little strange?"

Teresa laughed. "Of course it will. But who cares? Since I've come out of the closet as a psychic, a lot of people think I'm strange."

Amanda crunched another chip with hot sauce. The last few months of having Charley around had been a nightmare. She couldn't imagine what it would be like to have spirits hanging around for years. "So you just recently started telling people about this gift, but you've done it all your life?"

Teresa shrugged. "I was five years old when my grandmother died and came back to visit with me. She was a gypsy, and she had the sight. I didn't know because Mother worked really hard to keep her quiet about it while she was alive. After Grandmother died, Mother worked really hard to keep me quiet. *What*

41

would people think?" She laughed. "If I had a dollar for every time I heard that, I'd be on a Caribbean cruise with no worries instead of trying to make a living reading Tarot cards and passing on messages from the dearly departed."

"I can totally relate to that. Not the part about talking to dead people, but the part about hearing your mother say, *What would people think?* When I'd ask why we cared what they thought, she'd get really upset."

Teresa nodded. "My mother too. *What would people think?* was all the reason she needed."

"Exactly! And although that wasn't enough reason for me, fear of my mother's wrath was, at least when I was young."

"I know! My mother's only five two, but she got her bluff in on me early."

The warm evening settled around Amanda and she found herself unexpectedly comfortable with the woman she wouldn't have dared speak to in high school.

The waiter returned and set a frozen margarita and a bowl of hot sauce in front of Teresa. Again she smiled up at him. "Thank you. We have a friend joining us. Would you please bring a drink for him too?" She waved a hand toward Charley.

He beamed. "Thank you, Teresa. That's real nice of you. I always enjoyed a good margarita."

The waiter left with Charley's order.

"I think the margaritas here are the best. What do you think, Amanda? Charley?"

"Uh, yes, very good." It had taken Amanda some time to get used to talking to Charley. It was going to take some more time to become accustomed to having a conversation with him and another person.

"Chili's has great margaritas too," Charley said.

"Agreed, and they have wonderful burgers. We should go there next time."

Next time? Though she hadn't given it a lot of thought, Amanda had sort of assumed the next time would be in a dark room with a crystal ball or a spirit mirror, something appropriate to encouraging Charley to *go into the light.*

Charley's smile grew wider. "I'm ready any time. I miss going out with friends."

Amanda refrained from reminding him that one of his evenings out with friends had resulted in the visit from Ronald Collins and the threat to her shop.

Teresa nodded. "You probably miss a lot of things of this world right now like eating and drinking and feeling the sun on your face."

Charley leaned closer to her. "Yes! I do miss all those things. This isn't what I thought the afterlife would be like."

He had recently plunged into a fresh batch of fried chicken in an effort to taste it and had only succeeded in chilling the entire batch. Amanda suddenly felt a twinge of sympathy for him. But only a small, short-lived twinge.

Teresa leaned over and patted his hand. Her fingers went through his hand and touched the table top, but Charley seemed pleased at the gesture. "You're at a very low level. You're actually stuck between the physical world and the spiritual world. Once you move on, you'll be happy and peaceful and you won't miss the material things of this world at all."

"I won't?"

"I know! I can't imagine not missing margaritas and that first cup of coffee in the morning and the way the rain smells. But all the spirits I talk to assure me that's the way it is. You'll get there."

"And you can help him get there?" Amanda asked. "Have you done this for other spirits?"

"Not yet, but it's a simple process." She waved a hand through the air. "As I said, I've tried to hide my gift for most of my life so I'm just now starting to get experience."

"Yeah, I don't remember you talking to dead people in high school."

Teresa smiled mischievously. "I did. I just didn't tell anybody. Remember history class when I kept getting in trouble for laughing?"

Amanda nodded though she didn't remember history class specifically. What she did recall was that Teresa had often been *in trouble* with all the teachers for laughing, talking, and being generally disruptive. While she drove the teachers crazy, the other students had loved her.

"We thought Mrs. Dawson had been there since dinosaurs roamed the earth, but before her, Walter Finfrock was the history teacher. He liked to hang around and make fun of her. You know how sometimes she'd get stuck on a subject and drone on and on in that monotone voice of hers? Well, Mr. Finfrock, looking sort of like Tim Conway in a 1940s suit and tie, would lie across her desk and pretend to snore. Sometimes he'd run his hands through that awful sprayed-in-place hair style of hers, and she'd reach up as if she could feel him."

Amanda laughed. "I wish I could have seen him too. It would have made it easier to get through that class. Mrs. Dawson was incredibly boring."

"I always wondered what kind of teacher Mr. Finfrock was. He might have been just as boring in his day, but he was quite entertaining from the other side. He knew I could see him, and I think he liked being acknowledged."

"Yes!" Charley agreed. "It's so awful when people ignore you."

Teresa turned to him. "I understand. Nobody likes to be ignored." She sighed. "But I have to confess, until Anthony and I broke up, I ignored a lot of the people who tried to talk to me. Dead people, I mean. I did my wifely duty and smiled and talked to the live ones who could help my husband make money and often pretended I didn't see or hear the others."

"Anthony also had a problem with your, uh, gift?"

"Big time. When I told him, he got very upset. Said it made me look crazy and he couldn't afford to have a crazy wife. He ordered me never to mention it again, not even to him. We did a lot of entertaining for his business. I always played Teresa the Cheerleader instead of Teresa the Medium. Now, all bets are off." She smiled, lifted her drink and took a sip directly from the glass rather than through the straw. "Love the salt. I can't imagine people drinking these without salt."

45

The waiter set a margarita in front of Charley. "Would you like to order now or wait for your friend?"

"I think we're ready to order. Fajitas?" Teresa asked.

"Sure. Fajitas."

Teresa handed her menu to the waiter. "Steak fajitas for two, extra guacamole." She looked at Charley. "And a plate for our friend who's running a little late, but we know he'll be here. He's on a diet so he'll just share our food."

The waiter left with their order.

Amanda was feeling much less antagonistic toward Teresa. In fact, she felt a sort of bonding with the former cheerleader. They'd both had to overcome backgrounds of propriety, and they'd both eventually succeeded in embracing the differences that got them in trouble when they were younger.

Or maybe that mellow feeling was just because she'd almost finished her first margarita. "So why did you come out of the closet? What happened to make you suddenly decide it was okay for people to think you're strange?"

Teresa wrapped both hands around her glass and gave a rueful half smile. "I wish I could say it's because I realize the world needs my gift or that my grandmother—who still talks to me sometimes, by the way, though not as often as she used to—convinced me I should be honest, but the truth is, money was the deciding factor. When Anthony kicked me out, I had to find a way to earn a living. I didn't have a lot of choices. I wasn't smart like you, Amanda. You have no idea how much I used to envy you."

Amanda almost choked on her drink. "You envied me?" The most popular girl in high school had envied her, one of the least popular?

"You were smart and funny and you had so much self-confidence. You said and did whatever you pleased and didn't let the latest fashions and hair styles rule your life. You just did your own thing and if the rest of the world didn't like it, that was their problem."

It wasn't exactly the way Amanda remembered her painful passage through high school, but if Teresa saw it that way, she wasn't going to argue with her. "I'm surprised. I just thought of myself as a geek."

Teresa laughed. "A geek? Whatever you want to call yourself, I always wished I had your kind of confidence, and now I do. I don't care who thinks I'm strange or different. There's not a big job market for former cheerleaders or former business party organizers, so I did the only thing I knew how to do. I hung out my psychic sign."

"You tell fortunes, read people's minds?"

"Sort of. Mostly I talk to people on the other side and reassure their relatives when they come to me. But I thought I should diversify, appeal to the largest possible market, so I read Tarot cards too. I'm a medium not really a psychic. I mean, I can't predict the future or read your mind or anything. Except I kind of can because of all the years I spent trying to please everybody and make everybody like me. I'm actually pretty good with those Tarot cards, but I think a lot of it is just reading people."

"So if you're only embracing your strangeness for the sake of money, are you going to go back into the closet when you get the money from Anthony's insurance policy?" Amanda wrapped her fingers around her margarita glass and tried to appear casual while watching Teresa carefully for signs of guilt.

Teresa sipped her drink and shook her head. "That's not going to happen. He took me off all the insurance policies and bank accounts the day he filed for divorce. He was really smug and pleased with himself when he told me about it. Even though his death doesn't help me any, I'm happy he's not going to benefit from all his careful plans. When they catch his murderer, I'm going to give the guy a great big hug."

At least Teresa wasn't showing any phony sadness. "Apparently he missed something. There's still a million dollar policy out there naming you as the beneficiary."

Teresa set her glass down, blinked a couple of times, and her lips tilted upward in a wide smile. "No kidding? Are you sure?"

"Pretty sure." Teresa seemed genuinely surprised about the policy. But there were plenty of times Amanda had trusted Charley, believed him when he lied to her. Unlike Teresa, her ability to read people probably wasn't the best.

"Well, I'll be damned." She laughed. "I'll bet he's spinning in the morgue right now at the thought that he left me some money in spite of his best efforts."

Amanda glanced at her empty margarita glass and the full one in front of Charley. "Are you going to drink that?"

He shrugged. "I guess not. Would you like to have it?"

"Thanks." She switched her empty glass for his full one. It was definitely a two-margarita evening. "Of course, if you killed your husband, you can't benefit from your crime."

Teresa cringed. "Not only could I not benefit, I couldn't stay out of prison, and that would not be fun. But I swear I didn't kill him." She turned to Charley. "Have you had any success contacting him?"

Charley spread his hands. "I don't know how. Everybody I see is alive. Tell me how to do it."

Teresa pursed her lips and regarded Charley thoughtfully. "You really are on a very low level, probably the bottom level. You must have been a really, really terrible husband."

He dropped his gaze. "I was."

"He was," Amanda verified.

"Then you should have no problem talking to Anthony. You two have a lot in common." Teresa lifted a large purple handbag, dug around for a couple of moments and produced a wallet. She took out a picture of a smiling dark-haired man and laid it in front of Charley. Amanda recognized the same smug, superior look on his face she'd seen on Charley's many times.

"This is him," Teresa said. "Look at his face. Focus on his name, Anthony Phillip Hocker. You can take the picture with you. Well, Amanda can take it. I certainly don't want it. In the middle of the night when it's quiet and dark, focus on the picture and his name, and you should be able to contact him."

49

The waiter arrived and spread the fajita feast on the table before them.

"I need another margarita," Teresa said. "And another one for our friend."

The waiter looked at the empty chair and the empty glass and nodded. His expression remained neutral as if he was accustomed to having invisible guests drink margaritas.

Amanda unwrapped a flour tortilla and topped it with meat, salsa, cheese, sour cream and a large dollop of guacamole. "Delicious," she mumbled around the food and looked up to see Teresa placing a small fajita on Charley's plate then building a second for herself.

Charley leaned close as if smelling the food.

The whole thing was a little strange, but she had to admit Teresa was gaining Charley's confidence. That should make it easier to send him on his way.

Amanda took a drink of the margarita she'd rescued from Charley. "So you can't talk to your dead husband but you can talk to your dead grandmother and the dead history teacher. Have you ever before had trouble reaching anyone?"

"Sometimes, if the person's already reincarnated. That's only happened a couple of times. Mostly my clients want to speak to somebody who's recently passed, somebody they knew—mother, father, husband—not their great great great grandfather who died a hundred years before they were born and has since moved on to another incarnation."

"You think maybe that's why you can't reach your husband? He's already reincarnated?"

"Ex-husband."

"You were still married to him when he was killed, weren't you?"

Teresa grinned. "Yeah, but I'm certainly not now. Maybe the divorce wasn't final, but his death was. He is definitely my ex."

Charley dropped his gaze to the table.

Amanda smiled. She liked Teresa. "I totally get what you're saying. Same thing happened to me."

"Except Charley was decent enough to stay around and tell you who killed him. I think Anthony's just avoiding me. I think he enjoys seeing me blamed for his death."

"Really? I thought when people got on the other side, they were more—I don't know—spiritual. They didn't hold grudges and have evil thoughts."

"Yeah," Charley affirmed. "I'm a changed man. I can't lie anymore."

Teresa swallowed the last bite of her fajita, wiped her fingers and reached for another tortilla. "They are supposed to be free of earthly vices. But I can't think of any other reason Anthony won't talk to me."

"Maybe he reincarnated super fast."

"Lord knows, he didn't get it right this time so he'll have to try again, but I doubt it would happen so soon. He needs time to reflect on what he did wrong this time, and there's a lot to reflect on."

Amanda selected her second tortilla. She was forced to accept that Teresa could talk to dead people since she talked to Charley. However, she was still having a little trouble wrapping her mind around the concept that Teresa talked to strangers, to the mothers, fathers, husbands and grandmothers of her clients, yet was unable to talk to her own husband. Ex-husband.

Teresa piled more meat and salsa on her tortilla. "Your grandfather wants me to tell you he's proud of you. He's been nagging at me since we got here."

Amanda froze with a spoon full of guacamole in mid-air. "Really? That's interesting since both my grandfathers are still alive."

Teresa frowned. "Are you sure? This guy says he's your grandfather and, as Charley said, they don't lie on the other side. Tall with curly red hair, says he died in a hunting accident when your mother was three. You've certainly got his hair."

Amanda's hand holding the guacamole dropped slowly to the table. "Does he—can you ask him what his name is?" Sunny's father had been killed in a hunting accident when she was three, but there was no way Teresa could know about her birth mother's existence, much less about that birth mother's father who'd been dead for over forty years.

Teresa sat quietly for a moment as if listening. "William Donovan, but everybody called him Don." She scowled and looked at Charley. "He says Charley did some bad things to your mother, but he forgives him. Does that make sense to you, Charley?"

"It makes perfect sense to me," Amanda said. That certainly dissolved any doubt she had about Teresa's abilities. Even if the woman had researched Amanda's family, she'd never have found the grandfather Amanda hadn't known about until she learned the true story of her birth a few months ago.

Charley cleared his throat and squirmed in his seat.

"He said for you to tell Sunny and Meg how much he loves them and that he's still around." She looked puzzled. "I'm getting the impression that Sunny is his daughter and Meg was his wife. Is your mother's name Sunny? That doesn't sound right."

The only mother Teresa could have known about was Beverly Caulfield. Amanda swallowed and cleared her throat. "It's her nickname." That was true. Amanda's birth mother's name was Suzanne, but everyone called her Sunny. "Tell him I will pass the message along to Sunny. To my mother."

"I don't have to tell him. He can hear you. He's pleased that you and Sunny are so close." Teresa smiled. "That's nice that you're close to your mother. So you got past the *what would people think* phase?"

Amanda thought about trading her once-again-empty glass for Charley's full one, but she had to ride her motorcycle home so that wasn't a good idea. "Not really. Sort of. How about your mother?" The question was a desperate attempt to change the subject. "Did you get past that phase with her?"

Teresa shrugged and grinned. "Not really and sort of. When Daddy lost all the money, he and Mother lost all their love. Funny how that works. She's in Kansas City with her second husband, and Daddy's in Florida with his third wife. Actually, he may be on number four or five by now. I haven't heard from him in a couple of years."

"So you're all alone now that your husband's dead?" Charley's voice was surprisingly soft and sympathetic. Maybe he was making some progress toward that next level after all.

Teresa laughed, the sound melodious and free in the gathering dusk of the summer evening. "I have friends, my created family. Trust me, that's a lot better than the one I was born into."

Amanda leaned back in her chair. Yes, she liked Teresa. So what if the woman talked to dead people and maybe killed her husband. She herself talked to her dead ex-husband and had often fantasized about killing him. Everybody had a few peculiarities.

She'd made a new friend, and that friend could help her finally get rid of Charley. For her part, she would do her best to help Charley make contact with Teresa's husband so he could tell Teresa who killed him. They'd help each other.

Who'd have thought the cheerleader she'd once envied and hated would one day become her friend? Even Charley's presence didn't diminish Amanda's pleasure.

When they had consumed the last fajita, the last chip and the last bit of guacamole, they split the check and left.

"Another bad thing about being like this," Charley said, "is that I can never pay the tab. I hate seeing you two ladies have to pay."

Charley had always insisted on paying the bill when they went out to eat. Of course, she often had to loan him money or a credit card in order for him to do so. But Amanda refrained from mentioning that part, from disturbing the serenity of the evening.

"This has been so much fun! We'll have to do it again even if Charley can't talk to Anthony." Teresa gave her a quick hug. "I'm parked next to your bike." She pointed toward a sapphire blue BMW convertible.

"Nice car. It looks like you."

"Thanks. It's fun to drive. The only good thing that came out of my marriage to Anthony."

As they started across the parking lot, Amanda noticed a tall bearded man wearing a baseball cap and sunglasses getting into a battered car on the other side of her bike. Who wore sunglasses at night? Was Ronald Collins following her? She was probably being paranoid.

Nevertheless, she made a mental note of the license plate.

Chapter Five

Shots rang out.

Amanda sat bolt upright in bed, going from sound asleep to wide awake in an instant. The clock on her nightstand showed three a.m.

With a rowdy bar down the street, it wasn't unusual to hear a shot or two in the middle of the night on Friday or Saturday, but this was Tuesday, the bar was closed, and the shots had sounded really close.

She listened but heard nothing. No more shots, no screams, no sound of running footsteps. Maybe she'd been dreaming. Much as she hated to admit it, the visit from Ronald Collins had spooked her a little. He was a creepy man.

"Want me to go check it out?" Charley appeared beside her bed.

"You heard it too? I wasn't dreaming?"

"I heard it."

"A car backfiring? Somebody shooting off firecrackers?"

"Sounded like gunshots to me. I'll go look."

Amanda swung her legs over the side of the bed, pulled open the drawer of her nightstand and took out her Smith & Wesson .38 revolver. "I'll go." If somebody was out there, she was better equipped to handle him than Charley was. She had a gun and a smart mouth. Charley could make somebody shiver if he went through that person. Not a lot of help.

She strode through her apartment to the front door, opened it and stepped onto the small landing. The street light was out. That could have been one of the shots. Even so, she could see well enough to be certain there was no movement in her parking lot, no sign of anybody. But somehow the warm night air felt ominous, as if something evil had passed through, leaving remnants of its essence behind.

She almost laughed at her own fancifulness. That damned Ronald Collins had creeped her out more than she wanted to admit.

Holding the revolver behind her back, she moved slowly down the wooden steps.

"I don't see anybody." Charley's voice behind her startled her, made her gasp.

"Thank you. I feel so much better now."

"You do?"

"No."

She reached the bottom of the steps. Nothing seemed disturbed. The door to the shop was intact and locked. She pressed her ear to the door but heard nothing inside.

She felt silly, standing outside in the middle of the night, wearing a red nightshirt printed with dancing M&Ms, and clutching a gun. She looked around, this time in fear of seeing a casual observer watching her and wondering about her sanity.

No one. The street in front of the shop was empty and still. The night was calm. Not even a night bird rustled in the leaves. Nothing moved in the shadows except Charley who was hovering under the big live oak tree a few feet away from the building. She had no idea what he was doing. Checking for fingerprints? Taking a leak? She was pretty sure ghosts didn't take leaks since they didn't drink anything, but there could be ghostly rules she knew nothing about.

She started back toward the stairs.

"Amanda, you need to look at this tree."

The tree stood tall and sturdy, leaves shimmering in the faint moonlight. Was Charley trying to create a romantic moment? "Okay, I see the tree. Now I'm going back to bed."

"No, come over here."

Amanda paused with one hand on the stair rail. "Why?"

"Because somebody shot your tree."

"What?" Amanda frowned but walked over to the tree.

Four large caliber bullet holes.

"Not a tight pattern," she said. "My tree assassin isn't a very good shot." Something to be grateful for.

"Yeah, I heard five shots. He missed once."

That might account for the street light even though it was nowhere near her tree.

She'd lived in that apartment for two years and nobody had tried to murder her tree before she met Ronald Collins. She couldn't rid herself of the creepy feeling that he'd been there recently, that he'd left an aura of evil behind.

Ridiculous.

Amanda stalked back upstairs, returned her gun to the nightstand drawer and settled into bed.

Sleep was elusive.

Nobody had been harmed, she reassured herself. A few bullets weren't going to hurt the big live oak. She hadn't seen anybody lurking around. Nothing to be concerned about.

Purely coincidental that Ronald Collins had showed up that morning and somebody shot her tree that night. As for the man she'd seen in the restaurant parking lot, he was just a bearded stranger wearing sunglasses. Maybe smoking dope and didn't want anybody to see his eyes.

She turned over and ordered herself to relax and go back to sleep. She was not going to let some creep like Ronald Collins make her paranoid.

Amanda woke early after a couple of hours of intermittent sleep. As she stumbled around in the shower, she cursed whoever shot her tree for disturbing her sleep and she cursed Ronald Collins, whether or not he was the shooter, for causing her stress.

She grabbed a robe and left the bathroom to find Charley waiting just outside.

"Rough night, babe?"

"Don't call me *babe*."

She dressed, strode to the kitchen and got a Coke. The bubbles fizzed over her tongue and down her throat, making her feel instantly better.

"I'd bring you chocolate donuts if I could."

She glared at him. "I can't prove you had anything to do with the shooting last night, but you did bring Ronald Collins into my life. Instead of thinking about chocolate donuts, you need to focus on getting rid of him. In the meantime, don't talk to me."

She dressed, warmed a piece of leftover pizza in the microwave then went downstairs and opened her shop. Dawson wasn't due for another half hour. She had time to relax, eat her pizza and drink her Coke.

She was seated at the desk with her feet up, finishing the last bite of pizza and feeling almost human, when she heard the front door open.

"You're early," she called. "I'm back here."

But it wasn't Dawson who crossed the room and appeared in the doorway to the small office.

Ronald Collins stood there holding a Starbucks cup, tobacco-stained teeth showing through his beard. She was pretty sure the macabre expression was supposed to be a smile. "I brought you some coffee. Thought you mighta had a bad night."

He was the SOB who'd shot her tree.

Amanda slammed her feet to the floor and stood, gripping her Coke can so tightly it bent. "My night was just fine, and I don't drink coffee."

"Looks like somebody used your tree for target practice. Woman living alone, shots in the middle of the night..." He shrugged and set the cup on the desk.

Amanda arched an eyebrow. "Really? I didn't hear a thing. I'm a very sound sleeper."

"You have a good day." Collins turned and left the room.

"You have a lousy day. I hope a meteorite falls on your head and burns that mess off your face."

He laughed and the front door closed.

"You okay?" Charley appeared by her side.

Amanda whirled on him. "No, I am not okay! What does that man think he's doing?"

"He's trying to intimidate you. He probably knows he doesn't have a legal leg to stand on, so he's planning to bully you into giving up."

Amanda slammed her Coke can on the desk. "I'm not intimidated. I'm mad. The jerk doesn't know me very well if he thinks he can bully me."

Charley looked around the room, not meeting her eyes. "He probably thinks you're somebody you're not."

"What does that mean?"

"Well, you know how men like to brag about their wives…"

"You bragged about me?" That surprised her and gave her a touch of mellowness toward him.

"I did, but that's not exactly what I meant."

So much for feeling mellow. "Then what, exactly, are you trying to say?"

He shrugged and continued to look across the room. "We sort of bragged about how we had control of our wives."

"Oh?"

"Yeah, they all did it, so I did too. We'd talk about how we did what we wanted and came home whenever we got ready and told our wives what to do, and they did what we said and didn't dare complain." He cleared his throat. "He thinks you're, uh…"

Amanda moved in front of him, forcing him to look at her. "He thinks I'm what? Weak? Easy to control? Malleable?"

"Yeah, except I don't know what that last word means."

"I wish you were still alive so I could kill you!" She stormed out of the office into the main area.

The front door opened. She grabbed a piece of twisted metal, formerly part of the fender of a wrecked motorcycle, and strode forward, wielding the makeshift weapon.

Dawson entered, his eyes widening when he saw her. "Uh, good morning."

Amanda dropped the piece of metal. "Good morning. I thought you were Ronald Collins coming back."

"Yeah, I saw him leaving. What did he want now?"

"To intimidate me into giving him my shop."

Dawson laughed. "He's in for a surprise."

"When you get a chance, I want you to check out a license plate number for me."

"The one on the car he's driving? I'll do it now. It won't take more than a minute or two." He moved past her into the office.

She followed him in, picked up a piece of paper and wrote the numbers and letters from the car outside the restaurant the night before. "Is this the plate on the car he was driving this morning?"

Dawson took the paper and read the digits. He shook his head. "No. It was completely different. I'll check both of them."

Amanda went to the refrigerator in the corner for another Coke. It was definitely a multi-Coke morning.

True to his word, within ten minutes Dawson looked up from the computer. "The car he was driving this morning is a 1987 Jeep Cherokee that's registered in the name of Janice Horne. She's the woman with the three kids whose address he's been using most recently. The one you gave me belongs to a car owned by Clyde Watson, a seventy-five year old man who lives in Waxahachie."

Amanda frowned. The man she'd seen last night was not Collins. She was being paranoid. "I suppose the man I saw could be seventy-five if he was in really good shape and dyed his beard." She moved around the desk to peer at the monitor. "Do you have a picture?"

"Sure." He tapped a few keys, moved the mouse around, and a Texas driver's license for Clyde Lee Watson appeared on the screen.

Amanda sighed. "Unless he's grown a beard, dyed it brown, lost a hundred pounds and grown six inches since that picture, this is not the man I saw, but I suppose anybody could have been driving his car."

"Yeah, he might have loaned it to his grandson or somebody. I don't see any reports of the vehicle being stolen."

"Can you find out if Ronald Collins is related to him?"

Dawson checked several more websites. "Not that I can find."

"Okay, I'm being paranoid. Thanks for checking. While you're on the computer, would you scan that paper Collins brought in and email copies of it to my dad and Sunny?"

"Sure."

Amanda went back to the regular shop area to install custom pipes on a bike. Dawson joined her a few minutes later.

Her cell phone rang. She laid down the parts, wiped her hands on an already greasy rag and pulled the phone from her pocket. Teresa.

"Good morning."

"That man wants me to come in for questioning again."

"That man?"

"Jake Daggett. This is the second time. Do you think I need to get a lawyer to go with me?"

Amanda drew in a deep breath and slowly released it. Damn! Jake asked her out but he was jacking with the one person who could make it possible for her to be alone with him, just the two of them, no ex-husband trailing along and making snide remarks. And she couldn't tell him. Not that it would matter even if he knew about Charley. He'd still do his duty as an officer of the law and all that stodgy stuff.

"When are you going in?" she asked.

"This afternoon at two. The only lawyers I know were friends with Anthony. Probably not the best pool to choose from when I'm suspected of murdering him."

"A friend of my dad went with me. You probably don't really need anyone if they're just questioning you. He hasn't accused you yet, has he?"

"No. He just said they had some more questions." She sighed.

"Then you're fine. If they start reading you your rights, you'll know it's time to lawyer up."

"That's not something I'm looking forward to. Well, I guess I'll just suck it up and see what they're going to throw at me."

Amanda thought about her interrogation following Charley's murder. Both her father and her lawyer had gone with her. Her lawyer had been more annoying than helpful, but having her father there for moral support had been of immeasurable value. "I'll go with you if you want me to," she offered impulsively. She could be supportive of her new friend and maybe win some brownie points to trade for Teresa's help with Charley.

"Thank you." Teresa sounded relieved. "I really appreciate that. I'll pick you up at one thirty."

"I'll be ready."

Amanda disconnected the call.

"You're just going because you want to see that damned Jake Daggett," Charley accused.

She would do whatever she had to do in order to get Teresa's help moving Charley on his way.

❧❧

Teresa arrived a few minutes past one thirty. She walked through the door of the shop and around the chaos of parts and bikes as if she were walking across a ballroom floor.

Charley darted toward her. "Hi, Teresa."

She smiled at him. "Hi. Sorry I'm late."

Amanda grabbed her purse from where she'd hung it on the handlebars of a Honda Goldwing. "Not a problem. Gave me the extra few minutes I needed to get ready. I hate it when people come early."

"Me too."

"Me too," Charley echoed.

Since Dawson was in the room, Amanda refrained from pointing out to Charley that being a few minutes late was quite different from being a few days late, which he'd often been during their marriage.

"Teresa, this is my assistant, Dawson. Dawson, Teresa. We'll be back in a couple of hours."

"Nice to meet you, Dawson," Teresa called over her shoulder as they went out the door. "He's really cute," she said when the door had closed behind them.

"Who?" Charley demanded. "Are you talking about that damned detective?"

"Daggett?" Teresa asked. "He might be hot if he wasn't trying to put me behind bars, but I was talking about Dawson."

Amanda had decided she liked Teresa, but she felt a sudden protective surge for Dawson. "He's very young."

Teresa grinned and shrugged. "I could be a cougar."

"Or not." Amanda opened the passenger door of Teresa's little convertible and got in.

Charley perched on the back of the seat. "This is going to be fun."

Teresa slid into the driver's side. "Yeah, it is a fun car. Too bad I won't have it much longer. Anthony always paid cash for everything, but apparently he financed this car. The bank called to tell me I've missed a payment. I think the jerk was planning this divorce long before he actually filed. Closed out my bank accounts and credit cards. Financed my car. Serves him right somebody offed him before he got a chance to see me squirm."

She started the engine and they zipped through the streets, sliding around corners and other cars with almost the same dexterity as a motorcycle. However, without a helmet, Amanda's hair flew in all directions.

When they reached the station, Teresa ran her fingers through her smooth, shiny hair, and it fell into place as though they hadn't just weathered a hurricane. "I love to feel the wind blowing through my hair. Don't you? It's such a feeling of freedom."

"I do," Charley agreed. "Well, in my case, it kind of blows through everything."

Amanda tried to run her fingers through her tangled curls but only made it about a half inch. She forced a smile. "Absolutely." Next time she rode with Teresa, she'd wear her helmet.

The three of them proceeded into the station and Teresa checked in with the receptionist.

When Jake came out, he stared at Amanda in surprise. "Amanda, hi, I wasn't expecting you."

Amanda looped her arm through Teresa's. "I'm here to provide moral support for my friend. I'm her attorney-in-fact."

Teresa smiled and confirmed the lie. "That's right. I signed a Power of Attorney this morning."

Jake looked as if he was going to protest but only shrugged. "Mrs. Hocker is welcome to have someone with her." He turned and led the way back to one of the rectangular interrogation rooms.

Jake sat on one side of the table and placed a file folder in front of him. Amanda and Teresa took seats on the opposite side. Charley sat next to Jake and peered at the closed file as if trying to see inside.

"Detective Ross Minatelli will be joining us. He's our forensic specialist."

They sat in awkward silence for a couple of minutes until the door opened and Ross walked in. He sat in Charley's lap.

Charley leapt up and scowled at Ross who was looking only at Teresa.

"That was rude," Charley said. He moved to a chair on the other side of Jake, settled into a semblance of sitting, and looked aggrieved.

Amanda ignored him and Teresa gave him a quick wink.

Jake made the introductions. Teresa smiled. Ross smiled. Electricity zinged between the two of them.

Amanda and Jake exchanged knowing glances. Ross was in lust again. It happened on a regular basis. Amanda wasn't sure how this one was going to play out. On a detective's salary, Ross couldn't possibly keep up with Teresa's lifestyle, but they might have fun for a while.

Jake opened his file. "Mrs. Hocker, you said yesterday that the last time you saw your husband—"

"Ex-husband."

Jake hesitated then nodded. "The last time you saw the deceased, Anthony Hocker, was Sunday afternoon at three o'clock."

"Give or take a few minutes, that's correct."

"You were in his home for approximately half an hour, and he was alive when you left."

"Yes."

"While you were there, did you have sexual relations with the deceased?"

Teresa's eyes widened. "No! I most certainly did not." She shuddered. "That's a disgusting thing to say."

"You were married to him for nine years. Surely you had sexual relations during that time."

"Sure, before I found out about Brianna." She frowned and shook her head. "I'm not following that act."

"We found hairs and body fluids on the sheet in the bedroom of the deceased's home," Ross said.

The expression Teresa turned on Ross froze the electricity between them in mid-arc. "I don't doubt that. Thank you for throwing *the deceased's* infidelity in my face."

Ross flinched, and his olive skin actually took on a reddish hue. Was he blushing? Had a woman just made Ross Minatelli blush?

"Would you be willing to give us a sample for DNA testing to rule you out as the woman in his bed?" Jake asked.

"I certainly will." She paused and frowned. "The man's a slob. He probably hasn't washed the sheets since I left."

"So you think we'll find a match to your DNA in that bedroom?"

"I did live there until a month ago, you know." She leaned across the table toward the two men, her eyes flashing dark fire. "But if you find a match, you need to check the age of that DNA. It's not going to be recent."

Amanda didn't like where this was going. She had to keep Teresa out of jail. Highly unlikely they made provisions for spirit progression sessions behind bars. She had to interrupt the process and give Teresa a chance to calm down.

She cleared her throat loudly. "Could I have a Coke?

Suddenly she had everyone's attention. They all stared at her as if she'd appeared in public naked.

"It's really hot in here, and my throat's dry. I don't think my friend can answer any more questions unless we have some Coke. One for each of us. I like mine cold but in the can. Teresa, do you want ice with your Coke or do you take it straight?"

Teresa blinked a couple of times, then the confusion cleared and she smiled. "I'd like mine in a glass with ice, please."

Jake and Ross exchanged glances. Ross stood. "Regular or diet?"

The men surrendered with dignity. Amanda was impressed. "Regular for me."

"I'll have regular too," Teresa said. "Thank you."

Ross left the room.

"That was clever, Amanda," Charley said approvingly. "You're getting good at this sneaky business."

Amanda shifted uncomfortably in her uncomfortable chair. It was a compliment, but not the kind she wanted to receive. She didn't want to become more like Charley. Surely the point of his continuing presence was to make him a better person, not make her a sneakier person.

Jake studied one of the papers in the file then looked up. "Were you aware that your husband...that the deceased was under investigation by the SEC?"

Teresa's eyes widened. "No." She bit her lip. "He told me we were broke, but I didn't believe him."

"Were you involved in his financial activities?"

"I gave parties and smiled at people and told them how wonderful Anthony was even after I realized he was a complete dick." Teresa gave a resigned sigh and leaned back in her chair. "But I don't suppose the SEC will believe that was all I did. If you don't get me for his murder, they'll probably get me for all his financial crimes. When I first heard he was dead, I thought that might solve a lot of my problems, but it looks like he's going to keep causing me problems even after his death."

Amanda shot a meaningful glance in Charley's direction. She could relate to that situation.

Ross returned with a can of Coke for Amanda and a glass for Teresa.

"Could I have a straw?" Teresa asked.

Ross actually seemed to consider it for a moment. "No."

"Okay." She took a long drink of hers. "This was a good idea, Amanda. These questions aren't as easy as the ones they asked yesterday."

Ross returned to his chair. Teresa smiled at him. He studied her uncertainly for a moment then smiled back. Lust prevailed.

"The deceased made regular large cash withdrawals from your checking and savings accounts over the last few months. Do you know what he did with that money?"

Teresa uttered a couple of swear words. "I should have known. Well, the jerk didn't give it to me. About a year ago he told me we were broke, cut my allowance to almost nothing and started selling off my jewelry."

"Sounds like he was being blackmailed," Charley said.

He knew all about blackmail, having been a participant.

"Did the deceased often conduct business in cash?" Jake asked.

Teresa shook her head. "You can keep asking me questions about his money all day, and the only answer you're going to get is, *I don't know.* Anthony was secretive about his money. Back when he was giving me plenty to spend, I didn't ask questions. When he told me we were broke and I started asking questions, he told me it was none of my business."

"So he emptied your bank accounts and sold your jewelry but you don't know what he was doing with the money. He wasn't making the mortgage payments. The house is going into foreclosure."

Teresa sucked in a sharp breath. "Maybe he really was broke. He loved that house. So did I. I decorated it." She shrugged. "But I'd rather the bank gets it instead of Brianna."

"About the only asset left is the million dollar life insurance policy in your name."

"Oh, yeah, Amanda mentioned that last night."

Jake's surprised gaze turned to her. "She did? How did you know about the policy, Amanda?"

Amanda tried to look innocent. "Internet." That was true. Dawson had found it on the Internet, not her, but she saw no need to elaborate.

Jake looked dubious.

"Anthony must have forgotten about it," Teresa said. "If he'd remembered, he'd have cancelled it. He told me I wasn't going to get a penny in the divorce." She slapped her hand on the table. "Now it all makes sense. We weren't going broke. He was hiding money so I couldn't get any of it!" She sat back and folded her arms. "I'm glad he got killed before he could enjoy it."

Amanda leaned close to Teresa's ear. "Don't say things like that. It gets you in trouble. Trust me on this one. Been there, done that."

Teresa gave a slight shrug and appeared unconcerned. Amanda wondered if she fully understood the situation. Perhaps she'd become so accustomed to having things come easily that she didn't realize she could go to prison.

"Did he keep any cash in that safe in the bedroom closet?" Jake asked.

Teresa flushed. She dropped her gaze then lifted it boldly. "Yes."

"Do you have the combination?"

"Yes."

"That safe is empty."

A thick silence filled the small room.

"Well?" Jake prompted.

"*Well*, what? Telling me the safe is empty is not asking a question."

Jake's brows drew together in a fierce scowl. Even Ross was no longer smiling. "Do you know what happened to the contents of that safe?" Jake demanded.

Teresa faced him defiantly. "Yes."

Jake's jaw clenched. Amanda found herself biting back a smile. Nice to know she wasn't the only person who frustrated him.

"Will you tell us what happened to the contents of that safe?" Ross asked, his tone quiet but deadly.

Teresa sat straight and met his gaze. "I took everything."

Chapter Six

Jake leaned so far across the table, his face was inches from Teresa's. "What did you take from the safe?"

Teresa folded her hands in her lap and thrust out her chin. "Cash. Five thousand dollars."

Amanda cringed. The woman was a terrible liar.

Ross lifted a dark eyebrow. "Is that all?" He knew she was lying too.

"What difference does it make? Anything in that safe was community property. Anthony was alive when I took it, and I was still legally married to him. I had every right to take whatever I wanted from that house."

Ross nodded. "Fair enough. When did you take it?"

"I just told you. I took it when he was alive and we were still married."

Amanda bit her lip to keep from smiling.

Jake did not seem to find Teresa's brashness amusing. "We got that," he said. "But could you be a little more specific?"

"I could."

"*Would* you be a little more specific?"

Teresa looked at Amanda for guidance. Drat. She'd come along for support, not for guidance.

"Don't tell them anything," Charley said.

Whatever advice Charley gave was likely to be bad. "Tell them everything," Amanda said.

Teresa looked from Charley to her then spread her hands on the table and drew in a deep breath. "Anthony called me that morning."

"For the record, which morning are we talking about?" Jake asked.

"The morning of the day he died. Isn't that the day we've been talking about?"

Ross nodded. "It is. Go on."

"He said he wanted me to come over to the house that afternoon and talk about getting back together. No way did I want to get back together with that jerk, but…" She paused and again looked at Amanda.

Amanda had no idea what the rest of that sentence was going to be, but she nodded anyway. Teresa might as well tell them everything. Cops had a way of uncovering secrets.

"When Anthony kicked me out, I had about twenty dollars in cash, less than a hundred in my checking account, no credit cards and no job. I knew he always kept some cash in that safe, and he didn't know I had the combination. The safe is in the bedroom closet next to the bathroom. So I figured I'd go over and talk to him for a few minutes, excuse myself to go to the bathroom, open the safe and take whatever money was there. And that's exactly what I did."

Jake and Ross exchanged enigmatic glances.

"Appreciate your being honest," Ross said. "We found your fingerprints on the safe."

"You were trying to trap her," Amanda accused. She'd been right. Nosy cops, always snooping around, trying to trap innocent people into guilty admissions.

Jake looked at her. "That's what we do. There won't be a problem as long as Teresa tells the truth."

Amanda folded her arms. She was pretty sure Teresa was telling some of the truth. All that business about *the truth, the whole truth and nothing but the truth* was highly overrated. Some details were inconsequential, had no bearing on the current situation, and were better left unsaid.

But she was a little curious about what part of the truth Teresa was holding back. Certainly something to do with what she'd taken from the safe. Probably a lot more than five thousand dollars. Amanda couldn't blame her for that. What if the cops decided to declare the contents of that safe as evidence and took it back from her? Amanda knew only too well what it felt like to have an ex-husband who'd already taken everything and then continued to take even from the other side. That brought to mind Ronald Collins and her situation. She shot Charley an angry look.

"What?" Jake asked, mistaking the direction of her gaze.

Amanda shook her head. "What what?" Yes, there were definitely occasions when it was not necessary or even smart to tell the whole truth.

"Are we done?" Teresa asked. "There's nothing else I can tell you."

Ross rested one elbow on the table and studied her intently. "Your husband asked you to consider a reconciliation?"

"That's right."

"What about his girlfriend?"

Teresa rolled her eyes. "He gave me the typical line of BS. He missed me, he'd made a mistake, it was all over between him and the bimbo, blah, blah, blah. I assumed he needed something from me, like signing over the rights to my left kidney or providing him with an alibi when he was cheating on the bimbo with a new bimbo."

"So you told him no?" Jake asked.

She arched a perfect eyebrow. "I told him I needed to go to the bathroom where I cleaned out the safe, stuffed everything into a tote bag, and left before he figured out what I'd done."

"You walked out with a bag full of money, and he didn't try to stop you?"

"I didn't give him a chance. I came out of the bathroom, waved and hurried out the door as fast as I could go."

Ross nodded. "The neighbors reported seeing you leave in a hurry."

"Of course those nosy jerks were watching. I parked in plain sight in the circle drive, as close as I could get to the door so I could run out and be gone before he caught me. I wasn't trying to hide anything, just get the money and get away."

Jake stared at her silently for a long moment. *Uh oh.* Bad cop was moving in. "You had a drink with him."

Teresa shrugged. "Sort of. He poured two glasses of wine and set them on the coffee table in front of us. Said he wanted to toast to new beginnings. I didn't trust him. I wasn't about to drink anything he offered me."

"You didn't trust him?"

"Duh. All of a sudden he's acting all contrite and sweet. He was up to something. When he offered me a drink, I figured he'd put drugs or poison in it. I pretended to take a sip then went straight to the bathroom and from there, out the front door."

Jake looked down at the papers in front of him then back up to Teresa. "So when you left, the glasses of wine were sitting on the coffee table?"

"Yes. Where were they when you found them?"

"In the trash, broken, but one did have your fingerprints on it."

"That sounds like an Anthony reaction. Get mad and break something."

Jake nodded slowly. Again he looked at the papers and said nothing.

"So, are we done?" Teresa asked again.

"Just one more question. About that million dollar life insurance policy..."

"What about it?"

"You said he must have forgotten to cancel it."

"That would be my guess. He cancelled all the other policies."

"But he didn't know about this one, did he?" Jake accused.

"Of course he knew. How could he not know?"

"You took out the policy."

"I took out one on his life, and he took out one on my life. We did it about six months ago when he first started complaining that we were going broke."

"He took out a policy on you?" Jake asked.

"Yes."

"Do you have a copy of that policy?"

For the first time, Teresa looked a little uncertain, but her voice was firm when she spoke. "No. I told you. He kept everything."

"We haven't found any policies on your life payable to him, just the policy on his life, payable to you. And, coincidentally, he's the one who's dead."

Teresa hesitated for an instant then lifted her purple designer purse, set it on the table and smiled. "A happy coincidence." She stood. "Anything else?"

Jake ran a hand through his hair.

Ross studied Teresa, his gaze inscrutable.

"Nothing else today," Jake finally said. "But don't leave town."

"I'm broke. I can't afford to leave town."

"You have five thousand dollars."

"I have what's left of that money after paying my rent and buying groceries."

Not to mention her handbag that looked new and expensive.

Amanda and Charley rose, and the three of them left the depressing room.

"He's looking at you," Charley said.

"Give it a rest," Amanda whispered.

"Oh, of course you'd think Jake was looking at you," Charley said. "I'm not talking about him. I meant Ross is looking at Teresa."

Teresa turned, looked back into the room, smiled and waved.

Amanda had to give her credit for having guts. Not a lot of common sense, but plenty of guts.

They walked to the car in silence though Amanda was bursting to ask Teresa about the contents of the safe.

When they were finally settled in Teresa's car in the shade of a big maple tree at one end of the parking lot, she asked the question. "How much money did you actually get out of that safe, and what else was in there?"

Teresa collapsed against the back of the seat and exhaled a long breath. She wasn't as composed as she'd appeared. "Do you think they knew I was lying?"

"Probably."

Charley leaned between them. "You're not very good at it. I could teach you."

Amanda groaned at Charley's words. "No, you couldn't. If you don't stop that sort of thing, you'll never get to the light." And she'd be stuck with him forever. No chance of taking a shower without looking over her shoulder. No chance of having any privacy with Jake. "Teresa, you'll be fine as long as they can't prove anything. So what did you really find in that safe?"

Teresa clutched the steering wheel and looked around as if to be certain nobody was close enough to hear. "Well, it was mostly cash, fifty thousand dollars in hundreds."

"Wow. That seems like a lot of cash to have on hand."

"It's more than he usually has, but he does like to flash the cash. I've seen him tip the valet with a hundred dollar bill if somebody else was there to see it and be impressed. But the other stuff I found is really interesting. I was in a hurry, so I just swept everything into my bag. I didn't know there was anything else until I got home and emptied it all out." She paused to let a man with a briefcase walk past her car.

"What else?" Amanda encouraged when the man was out of earshot.

"A flash drive and a phony passport."

"A phony passport?"

"Yeah, it had a picture of Anthony, but the name on it was Joe Richards."

"He was planning to skip town," Charley said.

Teresa nodded. "With that much money in cash and a phony passport, yeah, I think that's exactly what he was planning."

"No passport for the bimbo?"

Teresa shook her head. "Nope. Maybe little Brianna had hers with her."

"I think you need to tell the police about this."

"Why?"

"It could relate to his murder."

"Yeah, and I stole it from his house. How's that going to look? I had a right to the money. Half of it, anyway. But I probably didn't have any right to his phony passport. I don't want to get in more trouble than I'm already in. If I have to give back twenty-five hundred dollars, I can do that. But I'm not going to admit to anything else."

"You don't have to tell them how much money you took, but I really think you need to tell them about this other stuff. What's on the flash drive?"

"Just a bunch of garbage as far as I could tell. But I didn't get custody of the new computer. Maybe Windows 95 can't read whatever it is."

"I think we should let Dawson have a look at that flash drive."

"Why?"

Amanda threw up her hands. "Teresa, you're in trouble! Dawson might be able to figure out what's on it. We need to give the cops somebody else to investigate for Anthony's murder."

"Maybe the bimbo didn't have a passport. Maybe he was planning to leave town and not tell her. Maybe she killed him."

"Maybe. And maybe this passport and whatever's on that flash drive will point them in her direction."

"They're the police. They should be able to figure it out for themselves. That's what we pay them to do." She reached for the key to start the engine.

They wouldn't be able to talk while riding in a convertible at eighty miles an hour. Amanda closed her hand over Teresa's and halted her action. "You could go to prison. You need to do everything you can to avoid that."

Teresa took her hand off the key, bit her lip and looked at Charley. "If you could just talk to Anthony and ask him who killed him, we'd be able to solve that problem."

"I think I may have been close last night when somebody decided to murder our tree and interrupted me."

"Murder your tree?"

"Gunshots," Amanda explained. "One of Charley's old friends expressing himself. It's a long story. We can talk about it later."

"He's not my friend."

"Yeah," Teresa agreed, "friends don't usually come around in the middle of the night to shoot your trees. Did you call the cops?"

Amanda shook her head. "By the time I got outside, he was gone. I can't prove it was him, but he came by the shop this morning and said he noticed somebody had used my tree for target practice."

"It was Ronnie, all right," Charley said. "That's the kind of thing he does. He's trying to bully Amanda into letting him have her shop and apartment."

Teresa's jaw dropped. "What? You can't be serious! Why would he do that?"

"Because Charley signed my property over to him." Amanda gave Teresa a quick version of the Ronald Collins story.

"I paid him back the money," Charley insisted. "How was I supposed to know he'd do something like this?"

"He's a criminal," Amanda said. "What did you expect?"

"Charley," Teresa said quietly, "you have to stop making excuses and start taking action to right your wrongs."

"I'm trying!"

Amanda twisted in her seat to look at him in amazement. "You are? How do you figure that?"

"Well…" He looked upward toward the branches of the maple tree as if seeking divine assistance. Amanda was fairly certain that was not going to be forthcoming. He turned his gaze toward Teresa. "I'm trying to contact your husband."

"And what does that have to do with Ronald Collins or the other things you've done wrong?" She threw up her hands in resignation. "Fine. Whatever. So you think you got close to reaching Anthony?"

"Did you see him?" Teresa asked.

"No, not really."

"Hear him?"

"No. Maybe. Almost."

Teresa's forehead creased in a frown. "So exactly what happened to make you think you got close to reaching him?"

"Just…a feeling. I was doing like you said, staring at his picture and thinking his name, and it sort of felt like maybe he was there, but then the shots interrupted me."

"Hmm."

Charley couldn't lie, but Amanda figured he was fantasizing, trying to convince himself and Teresa he'd accomplished something he hadn't. Teresa knew it too.

If Charley didn't help Teresa, she might not help him move on into the light, out of Amanda's life.

"We'll work on it together tonight, won't we, Charley?" Amanda said.

"I'm trying! I really am," he protested. "I don't know how to do this. You should try being dead. It's not as easy as you think."

Amanda opened her mouth to tell him to stop whining, but Teresa spoke first. "How about we go to my apartment and I coach you with contacting the jerk?" She looked at Amanda. "Have you got another hour?"

"Sure. Dawson can handle things until I get back. And while we're at your place, you can give me that flash drive so I can take it to him and let him have a look."

"Okay," Teresa agreed. "Just don't tell anybody about the money."

They drove to a colonial style complex in the Oak Lawn area of town where Teresa pulled into a reserved spot in covered parking. The grounds were well tended, bushes trimmed and grass mowed. Mature trees shaded and sheltered the building. The rent would not be cheap.

"Be prepared," Teresa said, climbing out of her car and closing the door. "My apartment is tiny."

Compared to the houses Teresa had lived in before, her apartment might be tiny. Compared to Amanda's apartment, probably not so much.

They walked along a sidewalk to the back of the complex and entered through a door half hidden by shrubbery.

The living room was small but cozy. Bright pillows lay in a casual pattern on the white sofa and chair. Candles of different colors and shapes decorated the surface of the coffee table along with a couple of decks of bright Tarot cards and a glass bowl of crystals of different hues.

"Have a seat. I'll get us something to drink. Iced tea okay?"

"Sure." Amanda sank onto the sofa and Charley sat beside her.

Teresa disappeared into the kitchen.

"This looks like she knows what she's doing," Charley said. "With the spirits and all that, I mean."

"Obviously she has some ability. She can see you and she can see Sunny's father."

Teresa screamed.

Chapter Seven

Amanda ran to the kitchen with Charley close behind.

Teresa stood at the counter, paging frantically through a cookbook and swearing with vehemence and skill.

Amanda stopped in the doorway. No intruder wielding a knife or waving a gun. No bloody baseball bat lying on the floor. Nothing but a woman looking through a cookbook with a red plaid cover. "What's wrong?"

"Somebody's been in my apartment." Teresa pulled a slip of paper from the cookbook, clutched her chest as if in relief then looked up with a wide smile. "Thank goodness!" She waved the paper in Amanda's direction. "My grandmother's recipe for happiness. It wasn't in the place I usually keep it, and I was afraid someone had stolen it."

Amanda blinked a couple of times. Somehow Teresa didn't strike her as the kind of person who would have an emotional attachment to some schmaltzy recipe for happiness left by her grandmother. However, she would have never thought in high school that she would one day become Teresa's friend, so anything was possible.

"Read it," Teresa offered.

Amanda reached for the paper and read aloud the "recipe" written in faded blue ink and perfect penmanship.

Recipe for happiness
1 man to love you
2 children for you to love
1 dog who thinks you're perfect
1 cat who thinks he's perfect
1 house with 6 bedrooms
$1 million in a bank account in your name only

Teresa had a soft smile on her face, and her eyes were misty. "My grandmother was a special person. I miss her a lot."

Charley moved over to give her a comforting pat on the shoulder, a pat that went halfway through her shoulder.

Amanda frowned. "I thought you still talked to your grandmother."

"I do, but not very often anymore. The longer someone's been on the other side, the harder it is to reach them. They move on to other planes and visit here less often."

That gave Amanda hope that eventually Charley would be gone of his own accord. But *eventually* wasn't even close to soon enough.

Teresa tucked the paper back into the cookbook. "It belongs between the recipes for ginger snaps and oatmeal cookies. That's where Grandmother left it." She closed the book. "Just now I found it between bread and butter pickles and sweet pickles. Somebody moved it. Somebody's been in my apartment."

Amanda looked around the small room. It was cluttered in an artistic way…copper kettle on the stove, copper pans hanging on the end wall and several colorful items haphazardly but precisely strewn around on the beige countertop. Nothing looked out of place. "Maybe you moved it yourself accidentally. Why do you think somebody was in here?"

Teresa waved a hand at the counter. "Look at my canisters."

Amanda looked. Southwest style pottery decorated with bright colors. "Has their aura changed?" she ventured. "Can you see strange fingerprints on them?"

"Actually," Teresa said, "I can feel a lingering presence that doesn't belong here, and it's a dark presence. But I can give you more concrete evidence." She turned one of the canisters slightly then another and another. "Now the peppers are centered. They weren't before. Plus there's flour on my counter." She pointed a perfectly-manicured purple nail to an almost invisible white streak near the largest canister then spun around and pointed. "That drawer's not in there straight. It sticks and I have to wiggle it around to get it straight. My burglar wasn't tidy."

Who'd have thought Teresa would be a neat freak?

Amanda still wasn't convinced she'd been burglarized. "Is something missing?"

"I doubt it. I don't have anything worth stealing. No jewelry, no expensive stereo, computer with

Windows 95." Teresa gave a short laugh. "I'll bet whoever broke in was disappointed." She shivered and bit her lip. "But it creeps me out that a stranger was in here, touching my stuff. I'm going to throw out everything in those canisters, the flour first."

"Let's look around and see if anything's missing," Amanda suggested. "We probably ought to call the police."

Charley grimaced at that suggestion. "We don't need no stinking cops. I'll check the bedroom, make sure nobody's hiding in there. We can handle this." He walked through the doorway, his feet only a fraction of an inch above the floor. Showing off. Trying to look normal.

Amanda and Teresa went back to the living room where Teresa looked over everything carefully. "My crystals are out of order. Somebody touched them. I'll have to cleanse them."

This whole situation was eerily similar to what had happened to Amanda when Charley was murdered…an estranged husband killed, the widow's apartment searched. In Amanda's case, the killer had taken the gun he thought would incriminate him. So maybe now…

"Teresa, you do have something worth stealing."

"I do? What?"

"The money you took from your husband's safe."

Teresa shook her head. "Nobody knows about that except you, me, and the cops. The cops wouldn't have had time to break in before we got here."

"True, especially not with the way you drive. Besides, they'd just get a search warrant and do it legally. They're funny like that. But there is somebody else who may know about the money. The person who murdered Anthony."

Teresa's hand flew to her mouth. "Omigawd! You're right. I didn't take time to close the safe. If somebody came to kill him and steal the money—"

"And saw you leaving with a big tote bag—"

"It wouldn't take much to figure it out." Teresa sank onto the sofa, her tanned face noticeably paler.

"Nobody in the bedroom," Charley said, darting back into the living room. "I told you we don't need the cops. What's wrong, Teresa?"

"What did you do with the money?" Amanda asked. "I don't suppose you put it in a nice safe bank account?"

"No, of course not. It's in the trunk of my car. I need to have it handy when I go shopping."

Of course she did. Amanda sank onto the sofa beside her. "Do you think that's a good idea? What if your car gets stolen?"

"I usually bring the bag inside with me. I just didn't want to be tacky and haul around a bag of money while I have guests."

Good manners were more important than guarding thousands of dollars. Teresa hadn't completely set aside her mother's admonitions about propriety. "I think we can dispense with etiquette for the moment. Let's go get it. Now."

Teresa took her keys from her pocket. "If you'll go get the bag, I'll get that tea for us. Thank goodness I have a pitcher in the refrigerator since my teabags are in one of those canisters he contaminated."

"Don't you think you should check the bedroom and see if anything's missing?"

Teresa's smile returned. "What? You think somebody might steal my five hundred thread count sheets? Or maybe my Victoria's Secret underwear." She shuddered. "The jerk probably went through my underwear and touched everything. I'll check that while you get the bag."

Amanda took the keys and headed out the front door, pausing to check the frame for any visible signs of entry. Nothing. But the lock was old and simplistic. It wouldn't have taken much to get past it.

"She needs a deadbolt," Charley said, inspecting it carefully. "I could open that with a credit card."

"Yes, she does need a deadbolt." Amanda didn't ask whose door he'd opened with a credit card. She didn't want to know.

She went to Teresa's car, took the bulky canvas bag from the trunk and returned to the apartment.

Three glasses of iced tea waited on the coffee table amidst the Tarot cards and crystals. The glasses all matched.

Amanda sat on the sofa and took a big gulp. Cold, sweet, crisp...perfect. Was Teresa a good cook in addition to her cheerleading abilities? But they were friends now. Amanda wasn't going to feel jealous of the other woman's talents.

Charley wrapped both hands around his glass, lowered his face to the amber liquid then looked up and smiled. "Excellent."

Teresa sat on the floor and pulled the canvas tote bag over to her. "One of these days, Charley," she said, "you won't miss food and drink."

"Maybe we could get started on helping him to move to that higher plane soon. Like tonight," Amanda suggested.

"Sure." Teresa turned the bag upside down and several neat bundles of money fell out along with a passport and a flash drive.

Amanda looked at them, wondering if she should put on gloves before she touched them so she wouldn't contaminate any lingering fingerprints.

Teresa had no such reservations. She picked up the two objects and studied them. "Anthony used computers all the time. You could be right. There may be something on here that will lead the police to his killer."

"So we call the cops and tell them about the break-in, then you casually mention finding these items in this bag where they'd fallen in a pocket or something and you hadn't noticed them before."

Teresa lifted an eyebrow. "Tell them about the break-in? What am I going to tell them? That I sense a dark presence has been in my kitchen? That somebody moved my grandmother's recipe and dribbled flour on my counter? Nothing was taken. Underwear and sheets are all accounted for."

Amanda thought of how much grief the cops had given her when she'd tried to tell them someone had broken into her apartment and stolen her gun. "Up to you."

Teresa chewed her bottom lip for a moment. "I don't think so. I think I want to have as little to do with the cops as possible."

"Wise decision," Charley said.

"In fact," Teresa continued, "since you know those guys and they're not trying to pin a murder on you, why don't you take the flash drive and passport in for me?"

"Me? No. You should do it."

"You live closer to the substation than I do."

"Yeah, but..." Amanda hesitated. "Maybe we can trade services. I'll take in the passport and flash drive if you'll start working on Charley's progress into the light tonight."

"I will if he'll try to contact Anthony first."

"He will."

"I will?" Charley looked confused.

"Of course. Why not?" Amanda asked.

Charley nodded uncertainly. "It just feels a little strange, having you all talk about me like I'm not here."

"Please?" Teresa gave him a big smile.

"Oh, all right, I'm in."

"Okay, deal," Teresa said.

"Deal," Amanda confirmed.

Teresa handed the passport and flash drive to Amanda then began arranging her crystals and lighting her candles.

Amanda opened the passport and studied the picture. Similar to the one Teresa had given Charley, but in this one her husband looked grim. However, passport pictures made pretty much everybody look grim.

Joe Richards.

"Have you tried looking for bank accounts in this name?"

Teresa halted in her preparations for the ceremony. "No. Any idea how I'd go about that?"

"I don't, but Dawson will. I'll let him take a look at the passport and flash drive before I take them to the cops. The data must be important or Anthony wouldn't have put it in the safe."

"I guess so. Or it might just contain pornographic pictures of the bimbo."

"I suppose that's possible, but I'm thinking something a little more interesting, like maybe names of people who threatened his life."

Teresa gave a short, unamused laugh. "I don't think that list would fit on a flash drive. You'd need a couple of terabytes for that. He scammed a lot of people out of a lot of money."

Amanda held up the passport. "The bimbo may be on that list. Remember, there's only one passport here."

"I never liked her, but if she had the guts to kill him, I may have to rethink my opinion of her."

❧❦

By the time Amanda arrived home that evening, dusk was settling in. Dawson had closed the shop and gone home. She lifted the large overhead door and put her bike inside.

The evening had been interesting but not productive. Despite Teresa's best efforts, Charley had not been able to contact Anthony, nor had Charley moved even one inch closer to the light and away from her. She couldn't prove it, but she suspected he wasn't trying very hard to do either.

She slammed down the kickstand, got off the bike and removed her helmet. Charley was right beside her, a place he'd rarely been in life but always was in death. "Are you sure you're really trying to reach Anthony?" she accused. "Are you sure you're not worried Teresa will move you into the light and you won't be able to annoy me anymore?"

"Of course I'm trying. I don't know how to contact dead people. I'm not a medium. I don't know why she can't get hold of him. When I died, I came straight to you, Amanda. I didn't avoid you like he's doing to her."

"Come off it! You have no idea how you got stuck to me. You admitted you just showed up." Amanda pushed past him, locked the large door and went outside through the regular entrance, locking it behind her.

"That's true," Charley admitted, "but I think it was because I was worried about you and knew you'd need my help."

"I seriously doubt that." Amanda climbed the outside stairs to her apartment.

Charley floated up beside her. "You can't prove that's not what happened."

"No, but you can't prove it is. However, if what you say is true, you've already told me who killed you. That man is in prison and I'm safe, so why haven't you moved on?"

Charley didn't hesitate. "You still need me to take care of you. For one thing, if I wasn't here, you might get involved with that awful Detective Daggett."

Yes, Amanda thought. *I might. But I certainly won't with Charley around.*

৯৯

Amanda was sleeping soundly when her cell phone rang. It was still dark outside. Probably a wrong number. She pulled the pillow over her ears.

"It's Teresa!" Charley announced, and a cold feeling on her shoulder told her he was trying to shake her awake. "You need to answer!"

Teresa?

Amanda checked her bedside clock. Three in the morning. What was Teresa doing up at that hour?

She reached for her phone and put it to her ear. "Do you know what time it is? You better be dying."

"Close."

At the word and the tension in Teresa's voice, Amanda sat up, wide awake. "Define *close*. Are you hurt? Did the burglar come back? What's wrong?"

"No, the burglar didn't come back. I talked to Anthony."

Amanda knew Teresa talked to dead people. So did she, for that matter. Well, one dead person. But the news still surprised her. "You did? How did you finally reach him?"

Charley put his head close to the back of the phone as if trying to listen. Amanda turned her head away from him, but he moved with her. Couldn't even have a private conversation with her new best friend in the middle of the night.

"I didn't contact him. He came to me. I was asleep when I heard his voice."

A dull roaring noise sounded in her ears. Probably the result of Charley's head halfway through hers. "That's good, right? What did he say? Did he tell you who killed him?"

"No. He said he can't tell me until I give back the things I took from his safe."

"What? What use is he going to have for money on the other side?" Charley might yearn to taste food and drink, but he'd never said anything about money even though he'd been quite fond of it while alive.

"None, of course. But he says my taking the money and other things so close to the time he was killed has created some sort of link holding him between here and there."

"Wow. I have enough trouble dealing with the real world. I mean, this world. I guess there's a whole different set of rules on the other side. Have you ever heard of something like that happening before?"

"No, but remember, I'm just now starting to really explore my gift. I used to talk to dead people only when they talked to me, and I sort of accepted it as normal. I don't know all the rules. This is new territory for me too."

"So he *can't* tell you who killed him because you took his stuff or he *won't* tell you?"

"He says he can't, but I don't know if I believe him. I told him I thought somebody had been in my apartment and maybe that person was trying to steal the money. He confirmed that his killer had been there searching for the money and that I'm in danger as long as I have it in my possession."

Amanda shivered in the warm night air. "So if you get rid of it, how will the killer know you don't have it anymore?"

"Anthony will tell me his name and I can tell the cops so they can arrest him. I really think he's lying and he could tell me if he wanted to, but he's blackmailing me. He won't tell me until I give back the money. If he can't have that money, he doesn't want me to have it either."

"How are you going to give it back?" Amanda had a vision of Teresa handing the money to a ghostly figure of her husband, and the money falling through him to the floor.

"It's a symbolic thing. I have to take the money, the passport and the flash drive, put them in a bag that's all natural fiber and take it to the nearest Goodwill store exactly at midnight tomorrow night. Well, tonight now. I'm to leave the bag on the top of the bin along with a message saying all the proceeds should go to the poor."

"That's…interesting. What are the poor going to do with a flash drive and a phony passport?"

"Maybe somebody will donate a computer to go with the flash drive. As for the passport, it's—"

"I know. Symbolic. Did you ask him what was on the flash drive and what he was planning to do with that passport?"

"Yes. He admitted he was going to get out of the country because of the SEC stuff. He said that flash drive has encrypted pictures of him and the bimbo, just like I thought. He realizes now that he was a bad person, and he's sorry and all that. Blah, blah, blah. Too little, too late. He's ruined my life, and if I have to give back that money, I'll be even worse off. But I don't know what else to do. So I need you to bring me that passport and flash drive. We can't take it to the cops. I have to give it to Goodwill. I wonder if he'd know if I only left part of the money. Ask Charley what he thinks."

Charley moved away and shrugged. "She knows more about this other life stuff than I do."

"Did you hear that, Teresa? He doesn't know."

The roaring noise continued even though Charley had removed himself from her ear. Had he permanently damaged her hearing?

Teresa sighed. "I guess I'll have to do it. He refuses to even show himself until we get that little task out of the way. Said he couldn't. I don't know if I believe him. I think he's just being mean."

"Charley says he can't lie anymore. I would think the same restraint would apply to Anthony."

"You would think. But I'm not sure Charley was ever as evil as Anthony."

Amanda looked at Charley and thought about the things he'd done, including blackmailing her dad. "Oh, yeah. I think he was. I'll bring the flash drive and passport over this evening." As soon as she made a copy of both of them.

They ended the call, and Amanda sat on the edge of the bed with the phone in her hand, trying to take in everything Teresa had said. The woman's psychic abilities were genuine, so if she said she had talked to her deceased husband, she probably had. Amanda's only knowledge of the rules on the other side came from Charley, and he'd never been a fan of rules.

The roaring persisted even though Charley was all the way across the room. Had the wind risen in the night?

"I'm wide awake now," she said. "I'm going downstairs and copy the flash drive onto the computer then scan the passport."

"Good idea," Charley said. "Sounds to me like there may be something on there that Anthony doesn't want anybody to see, something besides nude pictures."

Amanda shrugged. "We already know about the phony passport and his plans to leave the country. What else could there be?"

"I don't know, but let's have a look and find out."

Amanda couldn't deny she was curious about the contents of that drive.

She pulled on a pair of jeans, crossed the room and opened the front door. For a moment she thought she'd talked to Teresa so long it was already morning and the sun was rising.

But a glance across the parking lot told her it wasn't morning. Her truck was on fire.

Chapter Eight

"Omigawd!" Amanda ran down the stairs in her bare feet. With each step down, each step closer to the fire, the temperature got hotter. The truck was several feet away from the shop, but the flames were shooting high into the darkness, licking ominously close to a couple of trees.

"The truck's on fire!" Charley shouted.

"Really? How can you tell?" Amanda darted to the shop door and unlocked it with trembling fingers. Was the fire going to reach her building? Was she going to lose her motorcycle? Her customers' motorcycles? All her clothes except the jeans and nightshirt she was wearing? Was she current on her insurance premiums? How could that stupid truck be burning? She never put much gas in it because she was never sure how much longer the ancient vehicle would run.

She snatched a fire extinguisher from the wall, started back out, then hesitated and darted around the bikes and bike parts to the room with the phone.

She set the passport and flash drive down on the desk, lifted the receiver and dialed 911, reported the fire, grabbed the fire extinguisher, and ran back outside.

"Hurry!" Charley darted dangerously close to the flames.

She rushed toward the blaze, hefting the fire extinguisher that suddenly seemed very small. "Be careful!" she warned Charley. "You're going to get burned." As soon as the words left her mouth, she realized how absurd she sounded.

He darted through the flames and back to her, screaming as if in pain, then smiling as though he'd performed a delightful trick.

"Not funny!" She lifted the nozzle of the fire extinguisher and pointed it at the truck.

By the time the fire truck arrived with sirens screaming, her extinguisher was empty and the blaze was dying down more from running its course than from her pitiful attempts to stop it.

The firemen made short work of dousing the remaining flames.

One man took off his helmet and gloves then approached her while the others packed up their equipment.

"Are you the person who called 911?"

"Yes. I own this place." She gave him her name, address and phone number, and he wrote it on a form.

"How did this fire start?" he asked.

"I have no idea. I was inside." She indicated her second floor apartment. "I heard a roaring noise, but I thought it was…" She looked at Charley who stood by her side. Probably not a good idea to tell the fireman she had thought the noise was her ex-husband's ghost with his head inside her ear. Did firemen have the authority to haul her off to the mental hospital? "I thought it was the wind."

"There's no wind."

"I was inside. I didn't know that."

He nodded. "Any idea how long the fire had been burning when you called us?"

"I don't know. Maybe ten minutes. Fifteen. A while but not long." How long had she talked to Teresa?

"The sound of the fire woke you?"

"No. I was already awake. I was on the phone with a friend."

He nodded again, seemingly unsurprised that someone would be on the phone chatting with a friend at that hour. "The fire marshal will come back tomorrow when things have cooled down to do an investigation. Your insurance company will need that information."

Amanda snorted. "Don't bother. I only had liability."

The fireman regarded her with a puzzled expression. "You don't want us to conduct an investigation? Vehicles don't usually spontaneously combust and burn for that long without a little help."

"He thinks you set it on fire," Charley supplied. "But don't worry. You had no motive since you had no insurance."

"You think I set it on fire?" Amanda exclaimed. "I didn't set it on fire! I have no motive since I have no insurance." Oh, dear. She was quoting Charley. "But it did seem like an awfully big fire for a truck that was mostly metal and had very little gas in it. I'm not sure it even had any oil in it. A big puddle underneath. I usually add oil when I get ready to drive it."

"Stop talking, Amanda," Charley directed. "Don't say another word until you have a lawyer."

"A lawyer?" she repeated, aghast.

"What?" The fireman's brows furrowed as his expression changed from confused to suspicious.

"I said, ah, lawdy," Amanda improvised. "I've lost my truck and have no insurance."

This man might not have the authority to haul her off to the mental hospital, but he looked as if he thought she needed to go there. "At least your building's safe. I'll file this as *turned over to owner*. Good night, ma'am."

As the fire truck drove away, Amanda surveyed the wreckage of her former wreck of a truck. Gradually her anger went from simmering to boiling as hot as the fire they'd just extinguished.

"Why would anybody want to burn that piece of junk?" Charley asked.

"My thought exactly. Why would anybody want to burn my truck and why would anybody want to shoot my tree? Could be the same person, somebody who wants me to give up my business without a fight."

Charley shuddered, the movement shimmery and a little creepy in the pre-dawn shadows. "Yeah, I can see old Ronnie doing something stupid like that. He doesn't have a very high opinion of women and thinks he can bully all of them. It works for him more often than you'd think."

"Why don't you go haunt him? Rattle chains and scare him and tell him there's a curse on this place."

"I'd never leave your side, Amanda."

Like he had a choice. "Then I'll find him, take you to him, and I expect you to do whatever you can to spook him. Remember, Teresa said you have to start righting your wrongs."

"I don't think it would be a good idea for you to confront him."

She whirled on him. "And I don't think it was a good idea for you to sign away my place to him! He's already threatened me, shot my tree and burned my truck. What's next? Shoot me and burn my building? I'm not going to wait until he destroys something important. I'm going to take the bull by the horns...or the arsonist by the balls, as it were." She turned and stomped into the shop.

"Where are you going? What are you going to do?"

"Something productive since I can't do anything about Collins right now and there's not much chance I'll be able to go back to sleep after all this. I'm going to make a copy of that passport and flash drive, and I'm going to see what's on the drive."

She went inside and sat down at the computer. After scanning the passport and saving it to the hard drive, she studied the covers and all the pages of the forged legal document carefully.

"I don't like the idea of giving this to Goodwill. There may be all kinds of clues to the killer that we can't see but Ross could, clues that might exonerate Teresa."

Charley settled on the edge of the desk, sinking a couple of inches into the wood. "I agree. I don't trust

Anthony. Just because I can't lie doesn't mean the same rules apply to everybody. Maybe all the rules are individual, based on what the person did in life. Telling lies got me killed so now I can't tell them. But maybe Anthony can tell lies. Maybe he's directing Teresa where to put these things because he has a partner who isn't dead and that guy is going to pick them up."

Amanda nodded slowly. "Much as I hate to admit it, sometimes you do come up with suggestions I'd have never thought of."

Charley smiled smugly. "Always glad to help."

Suggestions only someone with a criminal mentality could think of.

She was able to open the files on the flash drive with one of the obscure applications Dawson had loaded onto the computer, but the data yielded no secrets. Strings of numbers and letters. Nothing that made any sense. Nevertheless, she copied the contents onto the hard drive. Maybe Dawson could figure it out.

She leaned back in the chair and studied the flash drive and passport closely, turning them over and over in her hands. "I think we need to take these to the police instead of leaving them on top of the Goodwill bin and maybe giving them to a criminal. We can make copies for that. Teresa said it's symbolic, so as long as she thinks they're the real thing, she'll be making the gesture."

"I don't know if that's going to work," Charley said.

"Sure it will. I can get a flash drive that looks just like this one, and nobody will know the difference unless they actually check the data. But how am I going to replicate the passport? Maybe I can take it to Jake and let him study it then return it to Teresa."

Charley snorted. "Yeah, like that cop's going to let you have it back."

Amanda hated to admit it, but Charley was probably right. Once the cops got their hands on evidence, they weren't likely to return it any time soon.

"Tell me where I can find somebody who makes fake passports."

"Uh…" He dropped his gaze. "What makes you think I'd know somebody like that?"

"Do you?" She waited.

Charley cleared his throat and looked uncomfortable. "The only guy I know who could do that isn't very good at it."

"I don't care. All I need is a reasonably good cover. I can send your guy a copy of the picture, and the rest of the pages are just standard forms. I don't think Teresa will check it closely." She set the items back on the desk and bit her lip. "I don't like the idea of deceiving Teresa. But I don't think she understands how bad things could go for her. I'll give Dawson a chance to look at these first. If he finds something we can use, I'll tell the cops about it but I'll give the passport and the drive back to Teresa. If Dawson doesn't find anything, I have to give them to the cops in the hopes they can find something. This may be Teresa's only chance."

"You're going to trust those cops? I just hope you won't feel too guilty if Anthony won't tell Teresa who killed him and she goes to prison."

"I wish you were still alive so I could slap you. You're the one who pointed out that Anthony's spirit may not be trustworthy."

Charley put his hands in the vicinity of his pockets and tried to look trustworthy. "He may not be, but neither are the cops."

"I'll keep that in mind. How do I contact your friend to make me a dummy passport? I hope he's not like your other friend Ronald Collins. I'd hate for him to mistake me for a tree and shoot me."

≈≪

"Bank accounts," Dawson said after spending some time alone with the flash drive.

Amanda set down the headlight she'd been working on and went to the door of the office. "Bank accounts? Plural?"

"Yes. Four of them. The routing numbers are on here, so it was easy to track them down. One in Switzerland, two in the Grand Cayman Islands and one in Cancun, all in the name of the guy on this passport."

"Can you tell how much money is in each account?"

Dawson nodded. "I should be able to. Some of these other strings of digits are probably passwords."

Amanda walked slowly across the room to stare at the computer screen. "Wow. If Teresa hadn't taken the contents of that safe and if Anthony hadn't been murdered, he'd be sitting on a sunny beach right now, having a margarita and feeling smug."

"Now Teresa can have all that money," Charley said. "She'll be able to buy a new house and make her car payments and not have to be a psychic."

Amanda would have liked to say something scathing about Charley's continuing failure to grasp the concept of honesty, but since Dawson was there, she framed her response as a generic statement. "I suspect the SEC is going to be interested in that money. Jake said they were investigating him."

Dawson nodded. "This could be a huge piece of evidence."

"What about the passport?"

He shook his head. "It appears to be a regular passport. Whoever did the work was good. I can't find anything on it other than the standard information." He took the flash drive from the USB port and handed it and the passport to Amanda.

"Thanks. I'll…uh…take these to the police and be back in a couple of hours. Maybe longer if I get, uh, detained." Like if Charley's friend didn't have the phony passport ready when she got there.

Amanda's trip to Charley's forger friend provided her with a reasonable facsimile of a passport. Comparing the two documents side by side showed that Anthony had more skillful criminal friends than Charley did, but it was adequate for casual inspection purposes.

Next stop was an office supply store where she bought a flash drive that looked like the original and an envelope for the phony passport and flash drive.

Guilt stabbed through her as she walked out of the store, guilt at duping her friend. But it was for Teresa's own good. Leaving vital evidence on the top of a Goodwill bin in the middle of the night just didn't make sense.

With Charley on the back of her motorcycle, Amanda rode to the police substation. Having him always around had been bad enough when she thought she was the only one who could see him. After meeting Teresa, she wondered how many other people could see him. Was the man on the corner looking at her because he liked her bike or because he saw the ghost riding on the back? Was the little girl she'd just passed pointing and asking her mother to buy her a motorcycle or was she asking her mother about the strange man on the back of the bike, the one who wasn't wearing leathers or a helmet?

Hester Prynne thought she had it bad, being forced to wear a scarlet letter. How would she have felt if she'd had a ghost tagging along everywhere she went, a constant reminder of her bad judgment in marrying him?

Amanda parked in the lot, pulled off her helmet and walked up the steps to the police station. The late morning was pleasant, warm and sunny, and she was going inside to make contact with an attractive man who seemed to find her attractive too. This could be an enjoyable experience…if her ex-husband didn't have to come along.

"We need to get back to your shop," he complained, dragging his feet through the floor. "You can just leave this stuff with the receptionist."

"I'd like to see Detective Daggett," Amanda said to the receptionist.

"It's not right to let Dawson do all the work at your shop while you fiddle fart around like this," Charley said.

Amanda gritted her teeth and tried to close Charley out of her sight and hearing. Not a good idea to get into an argument with a ghost while standing in the police station.

"Dawson's always ready to help you out, but sometimes you take advantage of his generous nature." Charley moved to stand in front of her.

Jake walked through the door, looked at her and smiled.

She felt her own lips turning up in a smile to match his.

Charley stepped in front of her, blocking her view.

She forced herself to walk directly through him and not to shiver at the cold, eerie sensation that action caused.

"I brought you something," she said to Jake. "Can we get a room?" *Oh, damn, did that sound as suggestive to him as it sounded to her?*

"Sure. Come on back." He held the door for her then closed it in the middle of Charley.

"That was rude." Charley shook himself and followed close behind her.

Jake moved ahead and opened the door to the interrogation room they'd been in the day before.

Amanda took a seat and put the passport and flash drive on the table. "These were in the safe when Teresa emptied it out."

"And you're bringing them instead of her because…?"

"I live closer than she does."

Jake arched a dark eyebrow.

"She doesn't want to get anywhere near you all. Can you blame her? You're trying to pin this murder on her."

Daggett picked up the passport and looked inside. The eyebrow arched higher. "Why didn't she say anything about this yesterday?"

"We found it last night when she dumped out the bag." That was sort of true. They had found it last night, just not for the first time.

"So Anthony Hocker had a phony passport. What's on the flash drive?"

"How would I know?"

He looked at her in silence, his expression somewhere between grim and amused.

"Bank accounts in foreign countries." She spread her hands. "It's proof that jerk was getting ready to skip the country."

Jake nodded. "The SEC was poised to come down on him big time. They figured he was getting ready to run, especially the way he emptied all his bank accounts. I really appreciate your bringing this to us. We can return the money to some of the people he cheated."

More guilt settled over Amanda. Maybe Charley had been right about giving the money to Teresa instead of telling the cops about it. "All the money? What about the cash Teresa took from the safe?"

Jake nodded again. "She'll probably have to give that back. All five thousand dollars of it."

Amanda could tell by the way he said it that Jake knew there had been more than five thousand dollars in the safe but he wasn't going to press the issue. A point in his favor for pretending to believe it.

Of course, if Teresa collected on the insurance policy, she wouldn't have to worry about money.

Unless she was in prison, in which case she wouldn't have to worry about money for a different reason. "The fact there's only one passport means Hocker wasn't going to take his girlfriend with him, so she probably killed him when she found out."

"Or Teresa killed him when she found out he was planning to leave."

Amanda slammed a fist on the table. "How can you say that? Isn't this proof of…of something?"

"It's strong evidence that Hocker was planning to leave town. You did the right thing, bringing it in."

Amanda shot to her feet. In this one instance and for all the wrong reasons, Charley had been right. She snatched the flash drive and passport off the table.

Jake scowled. "What are you doing?"

"Taking them back."

"You can't do that. This is evidence." He extended his hand. "Please give it back." His voice was calm, extremely calm, as if he were speaking to an irrational person.

"And what will you do if I don't? Arrest me?" That would serve Charley right for always hanging around. If she was arrested, he'd go to jail too.

The door opened and Ross stepped inside. "Got some results." He looked at Amanda and smiled. "Hi, Amanda. Jake, come see me when you get a chance."

"What did you find?" Amanda asked. "Have you got something new on Teresa's case?"

"Don't say anything!" Jake ordered.

Ross opened his mouth then closed it. "I'll catch you later." He backed out and closed the door behind him.

Amanda slapped the flash drive and passport back onto the table, picked up her helmet and strode out the door.

"Amanda…" Jake called after her.

She kept walking. Maybe Charley wouldn't have the chance to interrupt her date with Jake. Maybe there wouldn't be any date.

"I guess he showed his true colors," Charley said smugly. "I told you he wouldn't give you back Teresa's stuff. I warned you about him. You didn't want to listen to me, but I was right. I know I'm not always right, but I was right this time. I'm doing my best to take care of you. You can't trust cops anyway, and that Daggett guy has an evil look about him. Did you see the way he raised that one eyebrow? That's not natural."

"Really? There is not one freaking thing that's natural about you!" Whether or not Amanda ever saw Jake again, she desperately wanted to get rid of Charley.

Chapter Nine

After Charley's scolding about leaving all the work to Dawson, Amanda took back a pizza. She strapped it to the back of her bike and Charley sat on it, chilling it as he chilled everything he touched.

Dawson lifted the lid and inhaled deeply. "Smells wonderful!" He took out a piece but paused with it halfway to his mouth. "Ronald Collins came by to see you while you were gone."

Amanda sighed. "Of course he did. Did he mention the truck?"

Dawson shook his head, swallowed his bite of pizza and took a drink of Coke. "He said he had a friend who was selling fire insurance if you were interested. I told him if he showed up here again, we'd call the police. I think you should call them anyway and tell them what's going on. That man's crazy. He could set the shop on fire next."

"I suppose I should call the cops, but I don't have any evidence he's done anything except be obnoxious." And she didn't want to draw Jake's attention to any more oddities in her life. How many crimes could she be involved in before he decided a social life with her wouldn't be a good idea? "I don't think Collins will burn down the building since he seems to want the place. He's trying to scare me, but what he's done is make me angry." With a vicious movement, she yanked the tab on a can of Coke. It popped loudly.

Charley jumped.

Amanda selected a piece of the lukewarm pizza. "Why don't you take the rest of this to Grant? Go home early."

"No," Dawson protested. "We got in a new paint job today and I need to get started on it."

"Tomorrow's only a few hours away. Go home. Get rested up so you'll be able to deal with the extra work I'm going to dump on you."

Dawson left with a grin and the pizza. Amanda continued to work. Not the paint job, of course. That was strictly Dawson's specialty.

When the sunlight streaming through the west windows of the shop turned to a soft dusk, she set aside the greasy parts and wiped her hands on a towel.

"Are we heading to Teresa's now?" Charley asked, going through the motions of wiping his hands. Though he could no longer work on motorcycles, he often went through the motions while Amanda worked and, even more often, gave unwanted and incorrect advice.

"I'm calling her right now to tell her we're on our way."

She punched the number on her cell phone.

Teresa answered on the first ring. "I was getting worried. It's almost eight o'clock."

"We have plenty of time. He said you have to do this at midnight, right?"

"Yes."

"See you in a bit." She would wait until she got there to tell Teresa she was going to accompany her on the trip.

Amanda locked the shop and went upstairs. After a quick shower, she dressed and tucked the envelope containing the phony passport and blank thumb drive into her motorcycle bag.

When she threaded a belt through the loops of her jeans and added the holster holding her latest acquisition, a small Colt Mustang .380, Charley protested. "Why are you doing that? Are you planning to shoot Teresa?"

"I'm planning to go with her to the drop site." She smoothed her T-shirt over the gun. "How does it look? Am I printing?"

"Are you what?"

"Printing. Can you see the gun?"

"No, you just look like you're fat on one side."

"Thank you. I know I can always count on you to say the right thing." Amanda grabbed her leather jacket and headed out the door.

"Do you think you're going to shoot Anthony's ghost? Sometimes I worry about you, Amanda."

As Amanda continued down the steps, she thought of her father's oft-repeated words: *Never point a gun, loaded or unloaded, at anybody unless you're ready to kill that person, and when you start firing, don't stop until you run out of bullets.*

That advice didn't apply to the present situation. If she started shooting at Charley, she'd only succeed in blowing holes in her own building.

෧෧

Teresa was waiting with three glasses of red wine. "I'm so glad you're here." She sat on the sofa and lifted the half-full glass to her lips. "I'm freaking out about this whole situation. If I leave these things with Goodwill, Anthony might still refuse to tell me who killed him. I wonder if it's possible there's something on that flash drive that might lead us to his killer and get the cops off my case and he doesn't want them to have it."

Amanda set the envelope on the coffee table, took a seat on the sofa and lifted her glass of wine. "I thought about the same things. I had Dawson take a look at what's on that drive, and it's not pictures. It's bank accounts in four different countries."

Teresa shook her head but didn't look surprised. "That lying SOB."

"It would seem he doesn't have to abide by the same rules Charley does."

Charley, sitting on the sofa between them, looked up from sniffing his wine glass. "I don't lie."

"But he can still be deceitful and give false impressions and make up lies for me to tell," Amanda explained.

Charley opened his mouth as if to protest, then turned back to his wine sniffing.

Teresa lowered her glass to the table. "Anthony lied about what's on the flash drive. What else did he lie about?"

"I have…Charley has a theory." Give credit where credit was due. "He suggested it's possible Anthony's not interested in the passport at all. He's trying to get you to give somebody the money you took from his safe as well as the information to get into those bank accounts. I find it highly suspicious that he wants you to put the items on top of the bin rather than throw them inside. If you stick them inside, it would make it difficult for somebody to retrieve them, whereas if you leave them on the top, somebody can just stroll by and pick them up."

"Somebody?"

"His partner, whoever that is."

Teresa's eyes narrowed and her nostrils flared. "Probably the bimbo." She took a long drink of wine. "People on the other side worry about the ones they loved who're still here. For example, my grandmother warned me not to marry Anthony."

"I try to take care of Amanda," Charley said. "I worry about her. I watch over her."

Charley was getting awfully close to breaking the lying barrier.

"The bimbo is actually my choice for a murder suspect," Amanda said, "but I'd like to know who's going to pick up that stuff. It will give the cops somebody else to focus on instead of you."

"I don't know anyone else it could be except the bimbo. He didn't have any friends." She emptied her glass of wine. "It's possible that jerk may be so concerned about his bimbo that he's working from the other side to get money to her, even if it means I go to prison for murdering him. Not enough he jacked over me completely in this life, now he's doing it from the other side." She picked up the wine bottle and poured more into glass.

"We don't know that it's the bimbo. It doesn't have to be a friend, just a business partner, somebody who helped him run a scam."

Teresa's eyes blazed with dark, angry fire. "No, he wouldn't do this for somebody who was just a business partner. This has to be personal. It sounds exactly like something he'd do. He is such a dick. And yes, I'm speaking in the present tense. Even in the spirit world, he's being a dick. That man is going to have to reincarnate about twenty times before he even makes it to the first level. He'll probably come back as a goat next time. No, scratch that. Goats are nice animals. A cockroach. He's on the level of a cockroach."

It was a good thing Teresa was taking the angry route instead of the sad one. Anger worked much better than grief when it came to dealing with lying, cheating, dead spouses, but right now wasn't the appropriate time. They had to be calm and logical to make Amanda's plan work.

"Okay, here's what I think we should do," she said. "We put a fake passport and flash drive in a bag along with stacks of cut-up newspaper with a few dollar bills on the front and back and drop it off then hide and wait to see who picks it up."

Teresa nodded. "I like that idea. Catch the bimbo in the act. She killed him."

"Surely he wouldn't want to pass on his money to his murderer."

"I don't know. People are different once they're on the other side. Maybe it's so wonderful over there, he's forgiven her for killing him. Or maybe he's just so infatuated with her, he doesn't care if she killed him." She compressed her lips. "I don't think they have sex on the other side, but nobody's ever said one way or the other. That might explain a lot. I'll get some magazines." She set down her wine and went to her bedroom.

Amanda looked at Charley. "Did you forgive Kimball for killing you?"

Charley took a final sniff of his wine then sat upright. "I don't know. I wanted to see him in prison, but that was mostly because he was causing you problems."

So the bimbo could be both partner and murderer. That certainly put a new light on events.

Teresa returned with several magazines, a handful of rubber bands, a pair of manicure scissors and her purse.

She settled on the floor, took a few dollar bills from her wallet and tossed them onto the coffee table. "Only one pair of scissors. We can take turns cutting and bundling." She picked up a fashion magazine and began snipping viciously.

Amanda lifted the envelope containing the fake passport and flash drive from the coffee table. Guilt settled heavily on her shoulders. She liked Teresa. No matter how justified she might feel in her actions, she couldn't lie to her. She cleared her throat and Teresa looked up, eyes wide and trusting. The guilt settled into a painful knot in her stomach.

"I have to tell you something."

Teresa waited.

Amanda cleared her throat again. She could feel the blood rushing to her cheeks. "I gave the real passport and flash drive to the cops. These are replacements. I was afraid there might be evidence on the originals that would clear you, and Anthony didn't want you cleared."

Teresa laid her magazine and manicure scissors on the coffee table and studied Amanda wordlessly, her expression unreadable.

"I'm sorry!" Amanda lifted her hands to the sides of her face and pressed against her temples which were starting to throb. So much for having a new friend. "I didn't mean to deceive you. I know I should have asked you first but I was afraid you'd say no and then the evidence would be lost forever."

Teresa dabbed at her eyes and sniffed. "That is so sweet."

"It is?"

"That you were trying to help me and you told me the truth." She smiled, picked up her magazine and resumed clipping but with much less anger. "I already knew. Ross called earlier to ask me some more questions. He thought I knew you'd taken the items in. I didn't tell him anything different. I think when this is all over and they catch the killer, he's going to ask me out."

"You knew all along? But you didn't say anything? You're not mad at me?"

Teresa continued to clip. "I was a little upset at first, but Ross mentioned how concerned you were about proving my innocence. I don't think anybody's ever stood up for me or taken my side my whole life."

She looked up from her cutting. "That means a lot, and if you felt you had to deceive me to do it..." She set an irregularly shaped, vaguely dollar bill sized piece of magazine on the coffee table. "Well, everything has a price."

Amanda looked at Charley who had remained atypically silent. He looked slightly smug at the justification of lying, his former favorite pastime.

"No," Amanda said. "That's not right. There's no price on my friendship, and lying isn't right. Well, lying to a friend isn't right. It's okay to occasionally lie to somebody who's trying to kill you and sometimes to the cops, but not to a friend. I need you to accept my apology."

Teresa stared at her for a long moment then smiled. "Okay. Deal. I accept your apology and your friendship. But I think I need your help cutting up these stupid magazines or we're going to be here all night."

Amanda picked up one of the magazines, tore out a page, folded it in half and tore, then repeated the procedure until she had a pile of rectangles no more imperfect than Teresa's versions. "We only have to fool him long enough to see who he is."

"Or she."

"Oh, yes, Brianna. Does she have a last name?"

"Brianna Carroll. And she looks just like that name sounds. She's skinny and blond and has a thin little nose."

"I hate skinny women," Amanda said.

Teresa grinned. "And I hate blond women with thin noses."

Amanda settled into her magazine shredding with a warm feeling. Sure, part of that feeling came from the wine, but a lot of it came from spending the evening with a girlfriend plotting the downfall of a cheating ghost ex-husband.

ॐॐ

A few minutes before midnight Teresa pulled into the alley behind the Goodwill store. Amanda got out of the car, leaving Teresa to drive around then come back and appear to arrive alone.

Amanda strolled casually along the sidewalk toward the corner, arms at her sides in case she needed to pull out the .380. She passed a laundromat, a discount store and several vacant units, scanning the area for suspicious people, especially skinny blond women with thin noses.

A man in shabby clothes sat on the curb, smoking a cigarette. He glanced up at her and mumbled something. She reached a hand under her T-shirt and flipped open the thumb break of her holster. The man looked down to the street again and continued mumbling. He wasn't talking to her. He could be talking to Anthony for all she knew.

Across the street a bearded man lounged against a vacant building, drinking from something inside a paper sack. Probably not a Coke. For a moment she thought it might be Ronald Collins. He had the beard, but he had too much hair.

She continued down the sidewalk.

Anthony certainly hadn't shown any concern for Teresa's safety when he'd instructed her to come to this part of town at midnight. Maybe in his current state he was unaware of the dangers of the physical world. Or maybe he was just a douche.

Before they left Teresa's apartment she had produced from her designer bag a small stun gun that she claimed would effectively disable anyone who bothered her. Amanda chose to put her faith in guns with real bullets, but at least Teresa wasn't totally defenseless.

"That homeless guy's looking at you," Charley said.

Amanda turned back to glare at the guy sitting on the curb.

He lowered his gaze and began talking to the street once more.

Amanda passed the Goodwill store, making note of the metal bin in front where Teresa was to leave Anthony's stuff before she continued across the street. After a final glance at her surroundings, she sat down on the curb.

She should have thought to bring a bottle of Coke inside a paper bag. That would have helped her blend in like the guy on the other side of the street. He still lounged against the building though he'd lowered his bag and was watching her. When her gaze settled on him, he looked away and again lifted the bag to his mouth.

She could really use a Coke. This whole business was making her nervous. She ducked her head, stared at the street and tried to look inconspicuous.

Charley sat down beside her.

A car pulled up and stopped.

"Here comes Teresa," Charley said. "She parked on the street. Now she's getting out of the car. She's walking toward the store, holding the bag out so anybody watching can see it. Oh, that homeless guy looked up and said something to her."

"Don't even think about it!" Teresa said loudly.

No zapping noise ensued. Teresa hadn't used her stun gun.

"He's talking to the street again," Charley reported. "You don't have to shoot him."

"I'm glad," Amanda whispered. "Shooting people makes such a mess."

"Yeah," Charley agreed. "Kimball made a big hole in my chest and got blood all over the apartment."

Amanda cringed. She hadn't been thinking when she'd made her snarky comment about shooting people, but it seemed Charley didn't mind discussing the gory details of his own demise. Further evidence that Anthony might not view his own death as a crime and could be turning his money over to his murderer. Or murderess.

"She put the bag on top of the bin. She's turning around and heading back to her car. She's driving away, going around the corner."

Now they waited. Teresa would drive a few blocks then double back and park in the alley until something happened or didn't happen and Charley summoned her. That was their plan.

Amanda shifted her position. Sitting on a curb wasn't comfortable, and her leather motorcycle jacket was hot when she wasn't moving through the air at seventy miles an hour.

128

"Somebody's coming," Charley reported. "It's a woman, a blond woman."

Amanda held her breath. The bimbo?

"I knew it!" Teresa shouted.

Damn! Shouting wasn't anywhere in the plan.

Amanda shot to her feet and whirled to see Teresa converging on the skinny blond woman who wore a very short skirt and knee high boots. She had a thin nose and big boobs. Had to be Brianna.

"Get away from me!" Brianna tried to sidestep Teresa's grasp but stumbled in her four-inch heels, falling into the lap of the man who talked to the street.

"Hey!" the bum protested, shoving Brianna away.

Teresa grabbed the woman's arm and yanked her up. "You're not getting one penny of that money!"

"Let go of me!"

The man rose and tried to separate Teresa and Brianna. "Don't do that!"

Amanda rushed up to intervene. "It's all right. They know each other."

"Women shouldn't fight." He grabbed Teresa's arm with a bony hand.

Teresa shook him off and focused on Brianna. "How dare you think you could get away with this!"

"Teresa, what is wrong with you? Stop!" Amanda clutched ineffectually at the battling hands of the women.

"Get away from me, you crazy bitch!" Brianna yanked at Teresa's silk blouse, ripping off two buttons. "No wonder Anthony left you!"

"I'm placing you under citizen's arrest for killing him!"

"Good job, Teresa!" Charley's hands struck each other in silent applause.

"I didn't kill him! You killed him because he dumped you for me!"

The man from the curb lifted his arms in a defensive gesture. "I didn't kill anybody."

Amanda tried to get between the two struggling women. "Let's talk about this. You came to get the money," she accused Brianna. "How did you know it would be here?"

"I came to see Anthony!" Brianna shrieked. "He loves me."

"He's dead. You killed him and now you want my money." Teresa struggled to hold Brianna's arms.

"He didn't say anything about any money. He said he has to move on and he wanted to see me one more time." Brianna freed one arm from Teresa's grasp and reached for Teresa's hair but caught Amanda's instead.

"Ouch!"

"He couldn't have told you that!" Teresa shouted. "You can't talk to dead people. I'm the one who talks to dead people."

"You talk to dead people?" the bum asked, his dilated pupils becoming even more dilated.

Brianna released Amanda's hair, jutted her chin and looked down her thin nose at Teresa. "Well, he did. His spirit came to me last night and told me to meet him here, but you ruined everything. I hate you!"

"I hate you more!" Teresa lunged for the girl's throat.

Amanda wedged herself between the two of them.

"He must have talked to her or she wouldn't be here." Amanda turned to Brianna. "But Teresa's right. You're not getting the money."

"What money are you crazy bitches talking about?" Brianna threw her arms into the air. "I came here to say goodbye to the man I love."

"You didn't come to pick up..." Amanda turned to gesture to the canvas bag on the metal bin at the end of the block.

It was gone.

Chapter Ten

Teresa's mouth fell open. She whirled on Brianna. "How did you do that?"

"She didn't." Amanda looked around but only the three of them, the bum who talked to himself and, of course, Charley. Even the man across the street who'd been drinking from a paper sack was gone. Probably terrified the crazy women were going to attack him.

Or maybe...

She looked at Charley. "Did you see anybody close to the bag?"

"No," Brianna, Charley and the bum who'd become embroiled in their fight answered at the same time.

"She's not talking to you," Teresa snapped at Brianna.

The man backed away. "I swear I didn't see anybody."

"I was watching you all." Charley grinned. "I always did enjoy a good cat fight."

"I'll deal with you later."

She was talking to Charley, but the bum flinched and turned to leave. Amanda laid a hand on his arm before he could get away. "There was a bag on top of that bin." She tried to sound calm and not freak him out any more than he already was. "Someone took it.

Did you see who did it? How about that man who was standing across the street? Do you know who he was?"

The bum snatched his arm away. "I gotta go. I got an appointment with the president." He turned and walked down the street in a shambling but hurried manner.

Charley darted after the man. "Are you going to let him get away?"

Amanda spread her arms. "What do you want me to do? Shoot him?"

At her last words, the man began to run.

"Damn it!" Amanda sank to the curb and put her head in her hands.

Teresa sat down beside her. "I'm sorry. I shouldn't have run out like that. I just got so mad when I saw that woman."

"I hate you!" Brianna shouted. "You killed Anthony so I couldn't have him and now you and your friend kept me from saying goodbye to him." She began to sob.

"Oh, stuff it!" Teresa ordered. "You'll wash those stupid false eyelashes off and you'll look like a raccoon."

Amanda rose. "Do you have a phony passport?"

"What?" One eyelash hung lopsided, and Brianna did indeed resemble a raccoon with her mascara smudged beneath both eyes.

"Your lover had a passport in a phony name and he moved all his money to foreign bank accounts."

Brianna's raccoon eyes widened.

"He was planning to leave the country. If you didn't have a phony passport too, I guess he didn't plan to take you with him."

Brianna sobbed more enthusiastically. Sufficient answer.

Amanda slid her cell phone from her pocket and resumed her seat on the curb. "We've got to call Jake."

Teresa shook her head. "No."

"Yes. I don't know what's going on with her." She nodded toward Brianna. "But somebody took the bag. This was a setup. It proves Anthony had a partner. He probably lured the bimbo here just to have a diversion so we wouldn't see his partner take the bag."

Teresa glared up at the sobbing woman. "He wasn't going to say good-bye. He didn't love you. He just used you."

"You're mean!" Brianna said between sobs.

Amanda located Jake's cell number and touched the screen to call him. "You'll get to see Ross again."

Teresa yanked the phone away from Amanda. "That's exactly why you can't call them. How are we going to explain to them that we came here in the middle of the night, delivering a bag full of phony money?"

"He knows you're a psychic." From the corner of her eye, Amanda saw Brianna start moving away. "Stop!" she ordered. To her astonishment, the woman stopped. "Stay right there."

The girl continued to sob but didn't move.

Teresa glanced at Brianna then turned her attention back to Amanda. "It's one thing for Ross to know I'm a professional psychic. But if he thinks I really talk to dead people and that Anthony told me to bring his money and passport to the Goodwill store, he's going to think I'm a nut job."

"It's okay for Ross to think you're a fake psychic but you wouldn't want him to know you're the real thing?"

"I guess that would be the same reason you haven't told Jake about Charley."

"Yeah, she does try to keep me a secret." Charley affected a sad expression, a bad imitation of a basset hound.

"Okay, I'll try to minimize the psychic factor, but we've got to either call in the cops or get out of here. By now whoever took that bag realizes it's not the real thing, and he may be coming back. And he's not going to be happy with us." Amanda held out her hand and Teresa returned her phone. "Besides, I'm not so sure it was actually Anthony who told you to do this. You said you didn't see him. How about you?" She turned to Brianna.

The girl wiped her eyes, smearing the black stuff more. One eyelash strip came off on her hand. "No, I didn't see him. It was dark. He woke me up in the middle of the night. I don't see why he'd talk to you when he loved me."

"You're obviously not familiar with the rules for spirits," Teresa snapped.

"And you are?" Brianna put a hand on her hip and sneered.

"She is," Amanda assured her. "So neither of you saw him. You only heard a voice. Are you sure it was Anthony's voice?"

"Of course I'm sure," Brianna said. "I know the voice of my beloved."

Teresa thought for a moment. "It sounded sort of like Anthony, but it was a little different. Hollow. Like it was coming from far away. Of course, he is far away."

"Has that happened with anybody before? That you could hear but not see the person?"

"No, but I never stole anything from anybody before. He said that was why I couldn't see him, because he was stuck in between."

"You stole from Anthony?" Brianna put both hands on her hips. "You really are the wicked witch!"

"Really?" Teresa mimicked Brianna, hands on her hips. "You stole a husband. What does that make you?"

Brianna thrust out her chin. "I didn't have to steal him. You were such a bad wife, you ran him off."

"That's enough." Amanda stepped between the women in an effort to avoid another fight. "I'm calling the cops so let's all be on our best behavior." She lifted her phone.

Teresa gave a resigned sigh.

"I'm not staying around for the cops," Brianna said. "I talked to them once and they weren't very nice."

"You were part of this. You need to stay here and talk to them," Amanda said.

"Let her go," Teresa said. "The cops know where she lives. They can track her down and haul her skinny butt to jail if they need to."

Brianna opened her mouth, but before she could continue the exchange of insults, Amanda waved an arm in her direction. "I'm tired of hearing it. Go. Leave. Now. Before I sic my private ghost, Charley, on you."

Brianna's smudged eyes widened and she turned and teetered down the street in her four-inch heels.

Charley chased after her, emitting melodramatic ghostly laughter.

"Do they have therapists on the other side?" Amanda asked. "He needs help."

"Freud's probably over there somewhere."

Amanda shook her head and dialed Jake's number.

"Amanda?" Jake sounded sleepy and she wondered, not for the first time, if he regretted giving her his cell number.

"Yeah, I'm sorry to call you so late, but we have information on the Hocker murder case. You and Ross probably need to come down here and check for trace evidence." She gave him a brief recap of the last few minutes.

"Why did you decide to leave the bag of phony money and passport on top of the Goodwill bin in the middle of the night?"

"Teresa got a message saying she should do it, and we thought we could trap the murderer or Anthony's partner or…somebody." It sounded pretty lame when she said it.

"Does Teresa have a copy of that message?"

"No, it was…verbal."

Teresa gave her a thumbs-up sign and a smile.

"All right. I'll call Ross and we'll be there as quick as we can."

Amanda disconnected the call. "They're on their way. You can tell them whatever you want about the voice in the night. I have no idea what Brianna's going to tell them."

Teresa sank down onto the curb again, put her elbows on her knees and rested her chin in her hands. "I have to tell them the truth."

Amanda sat beside her and Charley joined them in a semblance of sitting.

"Do you think Anthony really talked to Brianna?" Amanda asked.

"He must have or she wouldn't have known to come here. Maybe he planned to tell her goodbye and move on as soon as his partner got the money."

"Or maybe it wasn't his spirit at all. Maybe his flesh and blood partner pretended to be him. Maybe he was afraid you'd be here waiting for him, and he used her as a distraction so he could grab the cash and run."

"Really? You're having a problem accepting that Anthony's spirit is talking to his ex-wife and his mistress when Charley follows you everywhere you go?"

Amanda couldn't refute Teresa's logic but she couldn't quite accept it either. This whole situation reeked of earthbound greed.

કેન્જ

Twenty minutes later a dark sedan pulled up to the curb. Amanda and Teresa rose to greet Jake and Ross.

"Good evening, ladies." Ross took his backpack from the trunk and turned to them with a gleaming smile. "Dallas' finest at your service."

Jake stood for a minute looking around the area. "This isn't the best part of town to be this time of the night."

Amanda lifted her T-shirt to expose her weapon. "No problem. We're both armed."

"I feel so much better knowing you two are running around town with guns." He didn't sound as if he felt so much better. In fact, he sounded downright sarcastic.

"I just have a stun gun." Teresa displayed her small weapon that resembled a cell phone more than a gun.

Jake and Ross looked at each other but made no comment.

"Okay," Jake said, "what's going on? Why are we all here in the middle of the night?"

Ultimately there was no way around telling them that Teresa's dead husband had been their source of information. To their credit, neither Jake nor Ross showed any sign of being shocked by Amanda's recitation of the events leading up to their appearance at the Goodwill store in the middle of the night.

Teresa lifted her chin. "I'm a psychic. I often talk to spirits."

"But this could have been somebody alive," Amanda interjected. "Anthony's partner. The person who took the bag tonight."

"That would be the person who's going to be very disappointed when he discovers the contents are not what he's expecting," Jake pointed out. "Any idea who that person could be?"

Teresa shook her head. "Anthony worked with a lot of people, but he wasn't really close to anybody except, of course, the bimbo."

"If the bimbo..." Ross stopped and cleared his throat. "I mean, if Ms. Carroll was being used as a distraction, perhaps she knows who the other person is."

Teresa nodded. "I have no doubt she knows. All that BS about Anthony wanting to say goodbye to her...ha! She was here for the money, and she ran away as soon as she thought her partner had it. I'd really like to see her face when she realizes their little plan didn't work. She said you talked to her. Does she have an alibi? She was probably skulking around the day Anthony was killed and saw me with him so she killed him because she thought she was losing him."

"We have talked to Ms. Carroll," Jake assured them. "She has an alibi for the time of the murder."

"Then her partner did it. The man who took the bag. Are you going to dust that bin for fingerprints?" Teresa flung an arm toward the metal bin.

"I'll have a look, of course," Ross said. "But there are probably thousands of prints on that thing, and if this mysterious person just grabbed the bag off the top, he may not have touched anything."

Amanda flinched. "You mean we got you two down here in the middle of the night for nothing?"

"No," Jake assured her. "What happened tonight is important, and we need to investigate the scene. Can you show me exactly where the man across the street was standing?"

"And I need to know exactly where you placed that bag." Ross set his backpack on the sidewalk then brought out a camera and some plastic baggies. "There may not be fingerprints, but that doesn't mean the person didn't leave some sort of evidence behind."

Amanda, Jake and Charley walked across the street. "Do you think Ross believes Teresa's nuts because she talks to ghosts?" Amanda asked. Ross hadn't seemed particularly perturbed with Teresa's confession, and his eyes still twinkled when he looked at her. Amanda was actually more interested in Jake's reaction.

"Ross? No, a little thing like talking to dead people won't stop Ross from pursuing a beautiful woman."

"How about you? Would that sort of thing stop you from pursuing a woman?"

Charley rolled his eyes. "Of course it would!"

Jake looked at her, his lips tilting up in a grin. "I guess that would depend on the woman. Have you been talking to Teresa's dead husband too?"

"What if I have?"

"Have you?"

"No."

"Aren't you going to admit that you talk to your own dead husband?" Charley demanded.

Time for a change of subject. Amanda pointed to the boarded up window of the building next to them. "The man drinking out of a paper bag was standing right there."

She left Jake examining the area and walked across the street to where Teresa and Ross were doing more talking and laughing than examining. Obviously he was sufficiently enchanted with Teresa's bubbly personality that it didn't bother him to know she shared that bubbly personality with ghosts. Jake hadn't given her a clue about his attitude regarding that sort of thing, but she suspected he might not be as blithely unconcerned about it as Ross was.

"Okay, you're right," Teresa said. "A lot of people came to our parties and got drunk and told Anthony how wonderful he was. But I wouldn't consider any of those people friends. They were just business associates. Any of them would have a motive to kill him if they heard about the SEC investigation or when they realized he'd scammed them out of their savings."

Ross snapped a picture of what appeared to Amanda to be a crack in the sidewalk. "We're looking into all those people, and there are enough to keep us busy for a while."

Teresa leaned close beside him as if she were fascinated with the crack in the sidewalk...or the man studying the crack. "What about the aliens?"

Ross stood straight, looked at her uncertainly and blinked a couple of times.

Amanda had the same reaction. She'd accepted Teresa's ability to communicate with spirits since she was able to communicate with Charley. But...*aliens*?

"You talk to aliens as well as dead people?"

"They're not really dead, you know. They've just left their bodies. And of course I talked to the aliens. Anthony was never around to give them directions."

"Directions? To get home to their own galaxy? Was the compass on their flying saucer damaged?" From the look on Ross' face, Amanda suspected they were getting close to the *she's beautiful but she's just a little too nuts for me* point.

Teresa threw back her head, and her light laughter filled the dark, empty streets. "No, silly! I mean illegal aliens, like from Mexico. About a year ago Anthony fired our lawn service and started hiring illegal aliens for the yard work. He said he was doing it to help the men. He let them live in the guest quarters and paid them a small salary in cash. I thought maybe he was trying to become a better person so I worked with the first one to help him get his citizenship." She shuddered. "But when Anthony found out, he threw one of his tantrums. Told me to stick to shopping and mind my own business."

"Do you have names for these people? Contact numbers? Relatives?"

Jake had come up behind her and was holding his small notebook and pen.

"There were three of them, and Anthony called each of them Juan. I thought that was rude, but Anthony was a rude person. The men had names, and I do know them."

"How about other employees? Housekeeper? Pool boy? Chauffeur?" Ross asked. He had his own little pen and notebook. If somebody could get the contract to sell small notebooks and pens to cops, they could rake in a bundle.

"Don't be silly. We weren't that wealthy. I had a housekeeping service and a pool service. They came

143

once a week. Well, the pool service didn't come during the winter, of course."

"And you had a lawn service until a year ago. What happened with that?"

"I have no idea. Anthony fired them one day and a few days later, Juan One appeared."

"What happened to Juan One?"

"His real name was Hector Garcia, and when Anthony found out I was helping him apply for citizenship, he fired him. Called him ungrateful."

"What about Juan Two?"

"Alberto Jimenez. He went back to Mexico. He started with us in November, and by January, he was ready for warmer temperatures. Anthony tried to make him stay, but I helped him sneak out in the middle of the night." She smiled. "It really upset Anthony when somebody he believed he owned escaped from him. I thought he was going to have a heart attack. He didn't have a heart, so that never happened."

Amanda tried to catch Teresa's eye, but she was looking only at Ross. Amanda stepped back and whispered to Charley, "Tell her not to talk like that."

Charley darted between Ross and Teresa. "Amanda says it's not a good idea to talk about your husband's near death experiences with such happiness when you're around the cops."

Teresa gave a slight shrug and continued. "Then came Juan Three. He told Anthony his name was Jose Rodriguez, but he told me later it was really Eduardo Vasquez. He didn't trust Anthony, and it wasn't like he had a social security card or a driver's license to prove who he was."

"What happened to him?"

"I don't know. He was there when I left, but when I went back after the murder to give him his final pay, he was gone. Probably left as soon as you all showed up. There's that ugly little word in there...*illegal*."

"We don't care if he's here illegally," Ross said. "We just want to know if he can give us some information about Anthony's murder. It sounds like you were friendly with this gardener. Any idea where he might have gone? Friends in the area? Family?"

Teresa bit her lower lip. "If you promise you won't do anything to Eduardo or his family, I'll tell you."

"We're homicide, not immigration," Jake assured her. "Maybe Eduardo can tell us something that will lead us to the murderer and clear your name."

Smart man. Put it on a personal level.

Teresa exhaled a long breath. "Okay, I can give you an address for the family Eduardo visited every chance he got. Anthony didn't like for him to leave the property, but I took him to visit them several times. His cousin and her husband own the place. Isabel and Alberto Ramirez." She recited an address and both Jake and Ross wrote it down.

Jake's large hands dwarfed the small notebook but moved the pen fluidly as he wrote. He stopped writing, and she lifted her gaze to find him looking at her looking at him. Busted!

His lips parted in a brief smile, just long enough to make her feel they had shared a moment in the middle of the night in front of the Goodwill store.

He pushed his denim jacket aside to slide the notebook into his back pocket, and she caught a glimpse of his gun. Rumpled hair and a day's growth of beard, as if he'd just got out of bed—he had—combined with tight blue jeans, a quick smile and a gun on his hip. The whole package was pretty hot.

"I think we've done all we can here, and we've got a couple of new leads," Jake said. "Let's call it a night. Where are you parked?"

"Around the corner."

"We'll drive you there and follow you to see you get home safely." Jake and Ross strode over to their car. Jake opened the back door while Ross went around to lift the trunk and put his equipment inside.

"I don't want to get in that car," Charley protested. "I don't like being in the back seat of a cop car."

Amanda slid in.

"You can't get out," Charley said. "There aren't any door handles on the inside."

Amanda looked down. "Yes, there are."

Teresa slid in beside Amanda. "It's not a patrol car. Relax."

"Do you think Eduardo could be Anthony's partner?" Amanda asked.

"No way. He was a nice person and he didn't like Anthony."

"If he didn't like him, maybe he killed him."

"I don't think so. He was very gentle. He just wanted to make enough money to help his family back in Mexico."

Ross slammed the trunk. Soon Jake and Ross would be in the car with them.

"I have one more question," Amanda said. "Why did Anthony need a gardener in the winter?"

"How would I know? Why did he need a skinny blond bimbo with bad hair and a thin nose? Why does he need a passport and cash in the afterlife?" She drew in a deep breath and collapsed into the corner of the seat. "And what's he going to do to me now that I've betrayed him by giving him phony money, a phony passport and a blank flash drive?"

Chapter Eleven

Amanda parked her bike in the shop a little after two that morning. The night had been long, stressful, and a total disaster. They were no closer to finding Anthony's killer and keeping Teresa out of jail. Teresa was despondent and worried Anthony would do something to cause her more problems since she'd betrayed him. Charley, like Anthony, was stuck between levels, and this was probably not a good time to ask Teresa to help Charley progress up the spiritual ladder.

And if that wasn't bad enough, it was officially Friday, one day from her potential first date with Jake. Did it qualify as a double date since both Jake and Charley would be there?

It would likely be her last date with Jake. Taking an ex-husband along wasn't exactly proper etiquette even if that husband was dead.

"Brianna really is a skank," Charley said.

Ignoring him, Amanda locked the door to the shop and strode with heavy feet toward the stairs to her apartment.

"Something's wrong with Anthony that he chose her over Teresa." Charley matched her stride for stride, never out of her sight.

"Teresa's not as pretty as you, but she's all right. I like her. She treats me like I'm really here. She let me have margaritas and wine and fajitas."

And he never shut up.

Suddenly the weariness overwhelmed Amanda. She stopped halfway up the stairs to her apartment, dropped to the step, and pulled off her motorcycle boots.

"Amanda? What are you doing? Did you hurt your foot?"

"I'm tired. I'm exhausted, but I'm too stressed to go to sleep. I just need to sit here and relax for a minute." She peeled off her jacket and leaned back against the railing, drawing the warm night air into her lungs, trying to ignore the lingering scent of her burned truck.

Charley sat down beside her. "You have had a long day. I guess that's one good thing about being dead. I don't get tired anymore. But that doesn't make up for not being able to eat fajitas. Teresa said one day I won't miss food, but I still do. It's nice that Teresa always includes me, but I'm not really able to eat. I miss hamburgers and onion rings and a cold beer on a hot day. Not that I can feel the heat anymore. I even miss that. You think you don't like being all hot and sweaty, but it's better than not being hot, though I don't think I'll miss being cold this winter. I never liked the cold weather. Remember when we went down to Padre in December? You sure did get sunburned."

This wasn't exactly what she'd had in mind for a relaxing moment. Amanda focused on the pale sliver of moon riding high in the sky and tried to block the sound of Charley's voice. The night was pleasant, warm with a slight breeze. She took off her socks and wiggled her toes then drew in a deep breath and released it slowly. An owl gave its eerie call and a dog barked somewhere down the street. Peaceful night sounds except for Charley's irritating, never-ending monologue. Was there any way to drug a ghost and put him to sleep? He couldn't eat or drink so putting something in his food wasn't an option. Crush Ambien tablets in water and spray him?

Relax. Breathe in. Breathe out. Think happy thoughts—Charley floating upward into the sky, joining Anthony in a place where they could no longer communicate with the unfortunate women who'd married them.

A cold chill flashed through her arm and effectively pulled her from her happy place. Charley had tried to grab her arm.

"Amanda, are you listening to me?"

She sighed.

"Sh-h-h-h!" he warned. "I don't think he sees us. Reach down and slowly take out your gun."

That got her attention. "What?"

"Collins. He's over there by the trash bin. I wonder if he's going to set it on fire."

Amanda stood and looked toward the metal bin where a dark figure lurked.

"Now he's seen you. Shoot him. Quick!"

Anger washed over Amanda in a fiery deluge. Ronald Collins was the tainted icing on the poisonous cake of her awful day. She ran down the stairs, ready to take out her anger at Charley, Anthony, Brianna and everybody else on Ronald Collins. "What do you think you're doing?" she shouted at him.

"Your gun," Charley called.

The man looked toward her and Amanda saw the familiar bald head, beard and beady eyes. He glared at her but didn't move. His expression was defiant, challenging her for possession of her own place.

"Get off my property!" she shouted. She reached down, snatched up a rock and threw it. The rock clanged off the metal bin, missing Collins by inches.

His eyes widened. He turned and ran toward the street.

Amanda grabbed more rocks and chased him, tossing the rocks as she ran. One hit his back and he flinched but kept running until he reached his battered Jeep a block away.

He slid in and slammed the door just as Amanda caught up to him. The window was down and she reached inside, grabbing for his throat but catching only his beard. "Stay away from me!" she ordered.

"You're crazy!"

"Damn straight, I am, and you better not forget it."

He began to roll up the window, and she yanked her arm out just in time.

"Shoot him!" Charley encouraged.

"I'll shoot you the next time I see you," she called as he drove away in a cloud of black smoke.

A flicker of sanity returned and she realized she had just chased a man down the street in her bare feet, thrown rocks at him, then threatened to shoot him. She whirled on Charley. "Shoot him? You want me to shoot him? You want both of us to go to jail? What is wrong with you?"

"You could have at least pulled your gun and threatened him. I wanted to see his face when you did that."

"And what would I have done if he pulled his gun?" She spun around and started back toward her place, her legs suddenly wobbly as the anger ebbed. "I'm glad you never got a right to carry permit. We'd all have been in danger."

At least the area was deserted. No one around to see her acting as crazy as Collins had accused her of being.

"I don't see much point in having a gun if you're not going to use it," Charley grumbled.

"The only person I'd like to shoot is already dead, just not dead enough."

આ

When the alarm on her bedside clock shrieked, Amanda thought she must have accidentally set it a couple of hours early. Not so.

She hit the snooze button and lay back down.

She was just drifting off when her phone rang. With a groan, she sat up and looked at the display. Teresa's name flashed on the screen. It was not a good sign that Teresa was calling so early.

She answered and Charley crowded close to listen. Cold flooded her ear as he pressed against her. Her very own private air conditioner.

"Hi, Teresa," Charley said. "You'll never guess what happened here last night. Ronald Collins came by and Amanda chased him off. You should have seen him run from her!"

"Good job, girlfriend!" Teresa was properly enthusiastic, but she sounded as tired as Amanda felt. "Did you threaten him with that little toy you were packing last night?"

"She threw rocks at him."

"Charley—" Amanda tried to interrupt.

"She chased him down the street in her bare feet, throwing rocks at him. Wish you'd been here to see it." Of all the things she'd done in her life, apparently Charley was most impressed with her rock hurling ability.

Teresa burst into laughter. "In your bare feet?"

"In my bare feet. But I assume you didn't call to talk about my footwear. What's going on? You sound tired."

"I'm exhausted. Anthony came again last night."

"Too bad you didn't have Amanda there to run him off with a well-aimed rock," Charley said.

"I'm going to guess he wasn't pleased with our little switch." A year ago, Amanda didn't believe in ghosts. Now they seemed to be everywhere and involved in all areas of her life.

"He was angry, angrier than I've ever heard a spirit. He tried to hide it, but I'm all too familiar with that tone in his voice."

"What did he say?" Charley asked.

Amanda headed toward the kitchen to get a Coke. Charley matched her every step.

"Anthony ranted on and on about how he can't move on until I right the wrong of stealing his stuff, that the bond I forged when I did that is binding him to me and to earth. We have to get the real things back from the cops and turn them over to a charity, like he said the first time."

Charley groaned. "Oh, no."

Amanda opened the refrigerator, grabbed a Coke and popped the top. She took a long drink and did her best to block out Charley's voice and his presence. "You're the medium, so I'm sure you know more about this sort of thing than I do, but I think Anthony's actions are kind of suspicious. Obviously he's doing this so his friend can have the money and the list of bank accounts."

Teresa released a long sigh. "I pointed that out. I mentioned the disappearing bag and asked if his buddy was going to be there the next time to take the money. He said it doesn't matter what happens after I release the items. I have to make the gesture of releasing them since I stole them. He said since the items were his, he can give them to anybody he wants, and he doesn't want to give them to me."

"What a jerk," Charley said.

"Yes, he is," Teresa agreed. "I guess because he's stuck so close to earth, he hasn't had a chance to leave his earthly emotions behind and become a spiritual being."

"That seems to be happening a lot around here." Amanda pulled a chair away from the kitchen table and sat. Charley assumed a sitting position in the air with his head next to hers. "What did Anthony say when you told him you spent most of the money and I gave the passport and flash drive to the cops?"

"I didn't exactly tell him that. He wanted me to bring everything to another charity store *last night*. Well, early this morning. Can you imagine? He never did have any patience. I told him when that person broke into my apartment, I put the money in the bank and gave you the passport and flash drive for safe keeping."

Amanda took another long gulp of Coke. "I hope he doesn't decide to visit me. I already have my quota of ghosts."

"Hey!" Charley protested.

"I've always kind of enjoyed talking to people on the other side," Teresa said. "Having my grandmother visit is wonderful, and Mr. Finfrock made that boring class entertaining. It's rewarding to pass on a message from somebody's father or wife to the person left behind and give them peace about the death of their loved one. Some of the spirits I've come across are a little strange, but they're harmless, just confused. But now there's Anthony. Makes me wish I was like everybody else and lost touch with people when they died."

"I totally understand that. Visiting with the departed isn't like inviting a friend over and if he spills red wine on your carpet or says something rude, you can run him off and slam the door in his face."

"Yeah," Teresa agreed. "The spirits just come right through that door. They don't even knock. I really need to get rid of Anthony. We've got to get that passport and flash drive back from Jake and Ross."

"Good luck on that," Charley said.

For once Amanda agreed with him. "That may not be so easy. What if you just tell Anthony to go away, that you're not giving him anything and you don't care if he's trapped between worlds?"

"He's not going away. I'll be stuck with him for the rest of my life. Believe me, that man knows how to torment. I'll probably never get another night's sleep. Spirits don't have to sleep."

"I know."

"You think Charley's driving you crazy by always being around? At least he's not trying to torture you or keep you up all night."

"She's right," Charley said. "I'm trying to help."

"Well, Anthony's not. He's angry at me, and dealing with an angry spirit is not fun."

Dealing with a helpful spirit wasn't much fun either. Amanda lifted her Coke to her lips and realized it was empty. "I already asked for the items back once, and Jake told me they're evidence. I have no idea how we're going to go about getting them, but since I'm the one who gave them away, I guess it's up to me to get them back."

"I have some ideas."

That did not surprise Amanda. "Okay, I'm listening."

"We tell the guys we want to talk to them about last night. When we get into the station, Charley can look around and find the items. Then one of us says we have to go to the bathroom, Charley shows us where they are, and we take them."

"You've been watching too many television shows. Come to think of it, I don't believe that plan would even work on a television show. Here's a novel idea. How about we tell them the truth?"

"The truth?"

"Yes, the truth, but we tell it in a way that it seems to be to their benefit." Damn. That sounded like something Charley would say. She had to get rid of him soon before any more of his bad habits rubbed off on her. "We tell them you got another message demanding the real thing, and if we deliver it, this will give them a chance to catch and question whoever comes to take it. Anthony said it didn't matter what happened to the items after you released them. It only matters that you release them. So you get rid of him, and the cops catch his partner who may be his murderer."

"That's actually a good idea. I didn't know you were capable of such sneaky tactics, Amanda. I'm impressed."

She laughed, and Amanda felt laughter bubbling to her own lips. Only Teresa could make a joke in the midst of murder, the possibility of going to prison, one angry ghost, one annoying ghost and her nebulous promise to get evidence back from a cop.

Chapter Twelve

By noon Amanda had consumed three Cokes and two cups of tea and was moving at warp speed. Between bathroom breaks she finished repairing a bike, contacted Sunny about initiating legal action to have the spurious document Charley signed declared invalid, and had Dawson print out the address on Ronald Collins' expired driver's license as well as the one for the woman whose car he was driving.

Sunny told her they needed an address to have him served with the court papers so they wouldn't have to do service by publication which would take too long. Amanda wanted the situation settled now.

"No guarantee he's at either of these addresses." Dawson handed her the paper with several lines of print. "If he isn't, I'll do some more searching."

"Thanks." Amanda looked at the addresses.

Charley looked over her shoulder.

"Be careful," Dawson cautioned. "That man is seriously nuts."

"I know he is, but I'm not too worried about a man who runs away from a barefoot woman throwing rocks."

Dawson laughed. "I wish I could have seen that. I'd run from you if you were throwing rocks at me."

"Me too," Charley said. "You were scary. You and me together, we can handle Collins."

You and me together. That reminder of her entanglement with Charley sent her to the refrigerator for another Coke. Besides having to deal with Charley, she'd need reinforcement for the next event. She had to call Jake and try to convince him to part with the evidence long enough to satisfy Teresa's annoying ex-husband.

Dawson went to the main area of the shop to work. Amanda sat down behind the desk and called the station. Neither Jake nor Ross was there. She was both relieved and disappointed. It would give her more time to construct a compelling argument for releasing the evidence and more time to figure out how to keep Charley from coming along on their date.

Jake and Ross were probably talking to Anthony's last gardener. Maybe he would give them some evidence to exonerate Teresa...if he was willing to talk to the cops.

Even if the man wasn't willing to talk to the cops, maybe he'd talk to the woman who'd befriended him.

She called Teresa.

"Hi, Teresa!" Charley said as soon as she answered, before Amanda had a chance to say a word.

"Hi, Charley. What's up?"

I can't shoot him and I can't lock him outside, Amanda reminded herself. "You said you took Eduardo to visit his relatives. So you were his friend."

"I tried to be. I took him to visit his relatives and he told me about his family. I remember a little of my high school Spanish, and I think that made him more comfortable talking to me."

"You're bilingual?" Charley asked. "You really are amazing."

"What did he tell you about his family?" Amanda asked.

"He has a wife and three sons in Mexico. Right now they're with his elderly parents who are not in good health, and they're living in complete poverty. Most days they don't have enough to eat. He sends them money regularly, and he's trying to save enough to go back and make a better life for all of them. I knew Anthony wasn't paying him much, so I gave him a little extra whenever I could. It wasn't a lot because that jerk was hiding money and telling me how broke we were when all along he was funneling money into those foreign bank accounts. If he wasn't already dead, I'd kill him."

"I know that feeling. So if Anthony had offered Eduardo enough money, he might have agreed to help with his plan to use that phony passport and leave the country."

"People will do a lot of bad things for money," Charley said.

He should know.

"Eduardo was a good man. I don't think he would have been a part of anything illegal."

"He came to this country illegally. Anthony could have offered him enough money to get back to his family, maybe start his own business. That might have overcome his scruples."

Teresa was silent for several seconds. "I guess it's possible."

"And maybe he saw a way to get even more money by killing Anthony and taking the cash from the safe. Only, of course, the cash was gone when he got there because you'd already taken it."

"No. Eduardo would not do that. No way. And if he did, why would Anthony's spirit be trying to get the money to him now?"

"Yeah, there are a few flaws in my story. I don't understand anything about the spirit world. Maybe Anthony's death was an accident. Or maybe it was self defense. Maybe Anthony tried to kill Eduardo, and now Anthony has to pay for what he tried to do to Eduardo."

"That's pretty far out."

"Okay, we have no way of knowing what happened, but it's possible Eduardo knows something. He did disappear about the time of Anthony's murder."

"Wouldn't you if you were in the country illegally and your employer got killed?"

"I sure would," Charley said.

Too bad Charley didn't have an employer. Amanda would consider bumping off the man just on that promise. "I tried to call Jake, but he and Ross are out of the office. They could be trying to track down Eduardo. If Eduardo is here illegally, he may not want to talk to the cops. However, if you were his friend, he might talk to you."

"He might. But what could he tell me?"

"I don't know, but it's the only thing we've got right now. We need something we can use for leverage to get Anthony's stuff back from Jake long enough for you to dump it and fulfill that silly requirement of his. Then they can have it back."

"Amanda, that's brilliant. Much better than my plan to walk in and steal the things back."

"You think?"

"I'll pick you up in thirty minutes, and we'll go see Eduardo. It'll be nice to talk to him again. I hope he's found a better job than the one he had with Anthony."

"Bye, Teresa!" Charley said. "See you soon!"

Amanda disconnected the call and lifted her hand to her forehead. She could feel a headache coming on. She needed one more Coke. Or one less ghost.

ॐ

"Are you jealous of Teresa?" Charley asked.

She'd told him to wait in the living room while she changed from her grease-stained jeans to a clean pair. He didn't sound as if he was very far away. Probably right outside her door which did qualify as being in the living room. Barely.

"I was jealous of her in high school, but not now. When you get to know people, you realize everybody has their own set of problems. I wouldn't want to trade my life for hers." She zipped her jeans then, since she was planning to look for Collins while they were out, added the belt and holster under her T-shirt.

When she walked into the living room Charley was leaning against the wall next to her bedroom door. "I mean, are you jealous because I like her?"

162

Amanda bit her lip to avoid giggling. "No, I promise I'm not jealous of your friendship with Teresa. But if you should decide you would rather live with her than with me, you're free to go."

Charley rushed to her side in a wave of cold. "No! You're my wife."

Amanda recoiled as if he'd thrown a knife directly into her gut. "Ex-wife."

"I'll never leave you as long as you need me."

She didn't need him, didn't even want him around.

Many times during their marriage she'd wanted to hurt him because he'd hurt her, but somehow it seemed cruel to hurt a ghost. Still, if he was staying around because he thought she needed him...

"Charley, you were never around when you were alive and I got by just fine. I promise I can manage on my own now. Don't you want to move into the light, sprout some wings, maybe be able to eat spiritual hamburgers?" She refrained from mentioning the possibility that he might sprout horns and a tail in the afterlife.

Charley shook his head. "Nope. Not as long as you need me."

"I don't need you." There. She'd said it. "I promise I don't. You're free to move on."

Charley stood very still and looked around him as if he expected the room to disappear while he was swept up and away. Amanda watched intently. Could it be this simple?

Of course not. Nothing happened. She was totally dependent on Teresa's help. Interesting how that worked out. She had to help Teresa get rid of her ex's ghost and Teresa had to help get rid of hers. Who'd have thought the cheerleader and the nerd would one day be working together as ghostbusters?

She pulled her hair into a ponytail in anticipation of riding with Teresa in her convertible at speeds in excess of all known limits except the speed of light.

They drove to Eduardo's neighborhood. Teresa's little sports car stood out from the older model sedans and vans in that area like a willow tree in the middle of a west Texas desert.

Amanda opened her door and slid from the car then checked to see if her ears had blown off. They were still attached. "Actually, this is not a bad neighborhood." The term *illegal alien* conjured up an image of a shack missing one wall with drug dealers and users smoking, dealing and taking random shots at each other.

The houses were small and old, some with flaking or faded paint, but the yards were tidy and well-kept. The small house they parked in front of was frame construction with immaculate white paint and a porch where two new boards gleamed against the faded gray of the others.

"It's probably better than where he lived before he came here," Teresa said.

They walked up the cracked sidewalk toward the porch. Windows with curtains fluttering in the breeze framed both sides of the closed door.

"Looks like somebody's home." Teresa knocked.

No sound came from inside.

"I'll check for you." Charley darted through the wall then came back almost immediately. "There's a woman in there. She came in from the kitchen, but she's just looking at the door. I don't think she intends to answer."

"That's probably his cousin. Isabel!" Teresa called. "*Està Eduardo aqui?*"

The door opened and a short, dark-haired woman stood looking at them, distrust and fear in her expression. "I do not know Eduardo. You have the wrong house."

"Isabel, I'm Teresa, Eduardo's friend."

For a long moment Amanda thought the woman was going to close the door in their faces, but gradually her fearful expression eased.

"Teresa? From the big house where Eduardo worked?"

Teresa smiled and nodded. "Yes. And this is my friend, Amanda."

The woman hesitantly returned Teresa's smile. "*Encantada de conocerla, Amanda.*" Her manners momentarily overcame her fear.

"*Encantada de conocerla, Isabel.* We're looking for your cousin, Eduardo."

Isabel looked from Amanda to Teresa, fear once again washing over her features. "Your husband, he was murdered. I saw it on the television."

"Yes," Teresa said. "He was."

"Eduardo had nothing to do with that."

"I know. I just thought maybe he saw something, overheard an angry conversation between Anthony and another person, anything to help us find the murderer."

Isabel shook her head and started to close the door.

"Please! They think I killed him. I just want to find out if Eduardo knows something that might help me."

"My daughter will be home from school soon. I have to go." Isabel closed the door.

"Your *abuela* wants you to talk to me," Teresa called after her.

Isabel's grandmother was speaking to Teresa? That was a stroke of luck.

Silence.

"Why can't I see her grandmother?" Charley complained. "I'm on the other side, but I can't see anybody else over here. You're on that side, and you talk to people over here all the time."

Teresa paid no attention to his whining. "*Su abuela Rosaria.* She's a short, round lady with gray hair, and she's always with you. She helped you find your car keys one morning when you were worried you'd be late taking...wait a minute...Rosaria, what's your great-granddaughter's name?...Rose, named after you. That's sweet. Isabel, she helped you find the keys one morning so you wouldn't be late taking Rose to school, and you knew it was her. You even thanked her."

Amanda was impressed. Teresa was really good at talking to the dead.

The door slowly opened again. "You can talk to my grandmother?"

"Didn't Eduardo tell you about my gift? Yes, I can talk to your grandmother. She wishes you could see her and talk to her, but she's happy to be with you. She said to tell you your mother and brothers in Mexico are fine, that your father is with them as she is with you."

Isabel crossed herself. "*Madre de dios!*"

"My ex-husband Anthony is on the other side too, but he's restless because he was murdered. If you can help me find his murderer, perhaps he can find peace."

Isabel hesitated then opened the door and stood back, inviting them inside by her gesture.

They entered the small living room. Isabel indicated a faded brown sofa. "Please sit. Would you like tea?"

"Thank you," Teresa said. "That would be lovely."

They sat on the sofa and Isabel left the room.

"That was a lucky break," Amanda said quietly, "that her grandmother asked her to talk to us."

"She actually told me to go away," Teresa whispered. "I just threw in the stuff Eduardo told me like the daughter's name and losing her keys and her father being dead and made up the rest. The grandmother's livid right now. She's very protective of Isabel. She's standing on the far side of the room, glaring at me. I'm sorry, Rosaria. It'll be all right, really. I won't do anything to hurt your granddaughter."

Charley perched on the back of the sofa between them. "You lied. You can lie. Amanda can lie. I can't lie, I can't eat fajitas, I can't drink margaritas, and you two are the only people who can see me."

"Ditch the pity party," Amanda ordered.

Isabel returned with three glasses of iced tea.

Charley heaved a deep, ghostly sigh. "No tea for the ghost. That's all right. I'm getting used to being ignored." He wasn't finished with his pity party.

Teresa suppressed a giggle. Amanda suppressed a scowl.

Isabel took a seat in the armchair facing them and leaned forward, clutching her glass of tea. "Where is Eduardo? I'm worried about him."

The conversation was not off to a good start.

"I don't know," Teresa said. "We were hoping you could tell us. My husband and I separated about a month ago, and I haven't seen Eduardo since."

Isabel shook her head. "Since you left, he doesn't come to visit so often. The last time I saw him was over a week ago."

Teresa bit her lip. "My husband was murdered a week ago today."

Isabel sat straighter in the chair and gripped her tea so hard her knuckles turned white. "What are you suggesting? That Eduardo had something to do with your husband's death?"

"No, of course not. But maybe he knows something. Maybe he saw something, and he's scared. Maybe he's hiding."

Isabel shook her head again, lines of worry creasing her face. "My daughter's birthday was last week. He promised he would be here if he had to walk the entire way. I worried when he did not show up Friday night. When he did not come Saturday or Sunday, I knew something had happened."

Amanda and Teresa looked at each other.

"This doesn't sound good for Eduardo," Charley said, echoing Amanda's thoughts.

"Did you call the police and report him missing?" Teresa asked.

"No. My husband and I are citizens, and my daughter was born here. But Eduardo, he did not come here the right way. We cannot tell the police."

"Maybe he went back to Mexico to be with his family."

"No." Isabel shook her head firmly. "The money he saved, it is still in his room here. Something bad has happened to Eduardo. He would not go home without telling us and never without his money. He worked very hard. He sent a little money home every week, but he was afraid to send much at a time. The mail down there does not always get things to the right people. So he worked and saved and talked about how things would be better when he got home."

Teresa sucked in her breath and went ghostly pale.

Isabel's comment was cause for concern about Eduardo's safety, but Teresa's reaction seemed a little over the top.

"Isabel," she said quietly, "I'm so sorry. Eduardo's on the other side. I just saw him."

Chapter Thirteen

Isabel gasped. Her hand flew to her mouth and tears hovered in her eyes. Again she crossed herself. "He's dead? Are you sure?"

Teresa nodded. Her eyes were suspiciously moist. "I'm sure. His image wasn't as strong as your grandmother's, but I saw him for a moment, and he spoke to me. He said, 'Send the money to Julia and tell her I love her.'"

Isabel took a tissue from the box on the coffee table and blotted her eyes. "Julia is his wife."

Teresa nodded. "I know. He told me about her. He loved her very much."

"Yes. He wrote her long letters every week." Tears streaked down Isabel's cheeks and she twisted the tissue in her hands. "How can I tell her that her husband is dead, that her children have no father?"

"I'm so sorry," Teresa said.

Amanda found her own eyes damp even though she hadn't known the man. Her heart broke for the woman in Mexico. How unfair that she'd lost a man she loved and Amanda couldn't get rid of a man she didn't love.

"Maybe he'll come visit his wife like I do," that man said, sensitive as always. "It's not like he's really gone."

"I cannot believe you just said that." Amanda gulped when she realized she'd spoken to Charley in front of a stranger.

Isabel blinked, astonished at Amanda's comment.

"She's not talking to me," Teresa said. "She's talking to the spirit of her dead husband."

Isabel nodded. "How comforting that you can talk to him. I have never been able to see the spirits of my beloved family. You are very blessed."

Amanda gave her a tight smile. This was no time to correct the woman, tell her that she was cursed, not blessed, with Charley's presence.

"I like her," Charley said.

"How did Eduardo die?" Isabel asked. "We must send his body back to his family so they can give him a proper burial."

Teresa bit her lip and looked at Amanda then back to Isabel. "I don't know how he died or where his body is, but I'll do what I can to find out."

The glance in Amanda's direction told her Teresa had just committed them both to the project of tracking down Eduardo's body. Not bad enough she had to retrieve items from the cops to make a ghost happy. Now she had to find a body. No wonder she'd never before had a best friend. The process could be exhausting.

Isabel's lips thinned. "Someone did this to Eduardo. He did not die natural. He was not sick."

Charley leaned forward. "Anthony killed him."

Teresa and Amanda turned to look at him. Amanda bit back a protest. Isabel was apparently okay with her talking to him, but she didn't think the woman would want to know about this unfounded accusation.

Charley smiled as if pleased to be the center of attention. "He killed Eduardo and then committed suicide out of remorse."

Amanda turned away from him. He was being so absurd, he didn't even deserve a response.

"I'm so sorry for your loss." The words sounded trite as Amanda spoke them, but she felt she should say something.

Teresa crossed the room and hugged the woman. "I'll let you know when I find out what happened to him."

Isabel nodded and again wiped tears from her eyes. "He was family. He lived with us for almost a year until he took the job with your husband and had to live there. He was no trouble. He took out the trash and helped me with the dishes. My little girl calls him uncle. She will be very sad."

A knock sounded at the front door.

"Excuse me." Isabel walked over to answer it.

"Isabel Ramirez?" The deep voice was familiar. The cops had arrived.

"*Si.*"

"We're with the Dallas Police Department. We'd like to ask you a few questions about Eduardo Vasquez."

Isabel burst into tears and stepped back into the room.

Amanda marched up to confront them before they could question what she and Teresa were doing there. She lifted her chin and looked down her nose at them through the screen door. "Way to go. You made her cry." The best defense—a good offense.

It worked. Ross blinked twice and took a step backward.

Jake wasn't so easily deterred. He sighed and ran a hand through his already-messy hair. "What are you doing here?"

Teresa moved up beside Amanda. "Visiting my friend, Isabel. What are you doing here?"

Teresa also subscribed to the good-offense theory.

Jake frowned. "We're trying to find your husband's killer. You gave us this address to talk to his gardener. Remember?"

She shrugged. "Oh, that. Well, you're wasting your time here. Eduardo's dead and Isabel doesn't know anything."

Ross' gaze narrowed. "What? Dead?"

Even Jake seemed taken aback by that comment. He opened his mouth to speak then closed it. His eyes darted from Teresa to Amanda and back again before he found his voice. "What do you mean, *dead*?"

Charley floated through the door and stood behind Jake, holding his hands above the cop's head as if mimicking large, floppy ears. "You sure picked a smart one this time, Amanda. A cop who doesn't know what *dead* means."

Amanda bristled. She didn't blame Jake for his confusion. She was angry with, but she snapped at Jake. "Departed. Gone to the other side. Probably murdered. It's going around."

"And you know this, how?" Jake asked.

"Teresa saw him and talked to him. Well, she saw his spirit and he talked to her."

"His spirit," Ross repeated. His dubious gaze focused on Teresa, and Amanda regretted blurting out the latest information about Teresa communing with spirits. Had they just crossed the line where strangeness overcame attraction?

"His spirit," Teresa confirmed.

"And he told you he was murdered?"

"Not exactly. We deduced that."

"I see."

Jake looked over their heads toward Isabel who stood behind them. "Mrs. Ramirez, can we talk to you?"

Drying her tears, Isabel stepped forward. "Teresa is correct. I can tell you nothing."

"You may be able to tell us more than you realize. I'd appreciate it if we could have a few minutes of your time."

Isabel hesitated.

"You don't have to talk to them if you don't want to," Teresa assured her. "But they're okay. I'll vouch for them."

Ross looked at her. "Gee, thanks for your support."

Teresa gave a mock curtsy. "You're welcome."

Isabel nodded and reached to push the screen door open. "If Teresa vouches for you, you can come in."

Jake compressed his lips into a tight smile. "We are so lucky to have Teresa on our side."

Teresa hugged Isabel then slipped out the door and waved as she passed Jake and Ross. "Happy to help. Maybe you can repay the favor sometime by returning some things you have that belong to me."

Subtlety was not high on the list of Teresa's virtues. In fact, it probably didn't even make the list.

Amanda turned to Isabel. "Thank you for your hospitality. I'm sorry we had to bring you bad news."

Isabel gave her a quick hug. "We must find Eduardo and return him to his family."

Jake and Ross moved inside, and Amanda brushed past them on her way out.

Jake touched her shoulder. "I'll call you tonight," he said quietly.

"I saw that! Get your hands off my wife!" Charley doubled his fist and swung at Jake's head. His fist passed straight through.

Jake blinked and shivered but appeared unaffected otherwise.

Amanda forced a smile and nodded.

The men went inside and she stomped down the sidewalk behind Teresa then slid into the car. "I...am...not...your...wife," she said through clenched teeth.

Teresa got into the driver's seat and closed the door. "Charley, I'm afraid she's right on this one. *Till death do us part.* That was the contract. I understand you're still a very real person with feelings and needs and desires, but the fact is, you are dead."

Charley perched astride the gear shift and looked hurt. "I thought you were my friend."

"I am your friend, but you've undergone a big change and you don't seem to be handling it well. Why don't you all come over to my place tonight? I'll try again to help you advance to a higher plane." She turned the key and the engine purred to life.

Amanda's smile was genuine this time. "That would be great."

"We can't," Charley said.

"What? Yes, we can."

"I thought you wanted to look for Collins. What was all the fuss about this morning, pushing poor Dawson to get addresses so you can find out where he lives, have him served, and call his bluff? Are you giving up on that? Are you going to let him bully you? Are you going to wimp out?"

"Zip it! We can check out those addresses this afternoon then go to Teresa's."

"Are we talking about the man you threw rocks at last night?" Teresa asked.

"Yeah. My…" She hesitated, unsure how to explain her relationship with Sunny without going into a lot of detail. "A friend is filing a lawsuit to challenge that stupid piece of paper my stupid ex-husband signed, but I need to find this guy so we can serve the papers. Otherwise we'll have to do service by publication, and that takes forever. I want this man out of my life *now*."

"So you're going out looking for this creepy guy, going to places in bad parts of town, talking to his criminal friends and cohorts?"

Amanda nodded. "That pretty much sums it up."

Teresa smiled. "Sounds like fun. I don't have any appointments this afternoon. I'll go with you."

"No," Amanda protested, "you don't need to go. I don't think this is going to be fun."

"What's the first address?"

"I don't remember," Amanda lied. "The list is back at my shop." Another lie. It was in her purse.

"I remember." Charley happily supplied the addresses.

Amanda compressed her lips and shot him a lethal glare. He'd do anything to avoid being sent to another astral plane, a plane where he might not be able to spy on Amanda and tag along on her date with Jake.

"Let's try the most recent one first." Teresa put Janice Horne's address into her GPS. "After we find Ronald Collins, we'll head back to my place and I'll work my magic with Charley." She slammed the car into gear and screeched away from the curb.

Charley's lips moved as if he were saying something…probably protesting Teresa's proposal to work her magic with him…but the wind from the momentum of the car stole his words. Just as well. He had nothing to say that Amanda wanted to hear.

Even with Teresa's driving skills, it took them almost half an hour to get across town to Collins' last known address.

The area made Isabel's neighborhood seem upscale by comparison.

Cars and remnants of cars squatted on the street and in the yards. However, Amanda did not see the ancient vehicle Collins had driven the night before. Toys, dead potted plants, a couple of bicycles, chairs and other objects littered the lawns. The only thing missing was grass. The houses were frame as they had been in Isabel's neighborhood, but these houses had flaking paint and sagging porches with rotting boards.

Amanda did not immediately get out of the car but sat for a moment taking in the house where Ronald Collins was living or had lived or had at least received mail. It was no better or worse than any of the others surrounding it, but she got a chill just looking at it. The peeling paint had once been some shade of green. Toys on the porch and in the yard suggested a small child lived there. Dawson had said the woman had three kids. The idea of Collins as a father sent a shudder down her spine.

She turned to Teresa. "Why don't you wait here while I see if anyone's home?"

"No," Teresa and Charley answered at the same time.

No point in telling Charley she hadn't been talking to him. Of course he'd come along wherever she went, and she had as much control over Teresa's actions as she had over Charley's. They were both going with her.

She opened the door and stepped out.

Remnants of an old sidewalk led from the curb to the front porch. Amanda shoved a yellow plastic tricycle aside and marched resolutely up to the torn, rusted screen door.

Teresa matched her every step. "No wonder that guy wants your shop. Nobody in their right mind would want to live here. Not that he's in his right mind. I mean, who shoots a tree?"

The sound of a television game show indicated someone was home.

Amanda knocked on the door.

The television sounds stopped.

She waited.

"He probably ran out the back door," Teresa said.

"Why would he do that?" Amanda asked though she had the same thought. "We're not the cops. We're just two women."

"And one man. I'll go see what's going on." Charley darted through the door.

Amanda looked at the place where he'd disappeared. "I have to admit, Charley's handy for checking behind closed doors."

"But the payout isn't worth the cost."

"Exactly."

"Don't worry. This is only temporary. You'll both be happier when he progresses a little further along the path."

Charley came back through the door. "A woman and three kids. No sign of Ronnie."

As if following him, a thin woman appeared at the door. She wore cutoffs and a stained T-shirt and balanced a crying baby on her hip. "Yeah?" She spoke from behind the screen and around the cigarette that dangled from her lips. Smoke curled about her face, into her brittle blond hair and the child's soft brown hair. Judging from the deep lines etching her angular face, she must be the grandmother, babysitting the kids.

"Uh, hi, my name is Amanda and this is Teresa." Oh, good grief! Amanda couldn't believe she was introducing herself as if this were a social visit.

"I don't know what you're selling, but I haven't got any money." The woman turned to leave.

"No, wait, we're not selling anything. You must be Janice Horne's mother."

The woman turned back with a scowl. "No, I'm not my mother. I'm Janice Horne. What do you want?"

Ouch! They were off to a bad start. Nothing Amanda said was going to make that comment any better. Best to let it drop. "We're looking for Ronald Collins."

Janice's eyes narrowed and she took a step backward. "Keep looking." The child's sniffling sobs became louder.

"We need to find him. We're friends of his." Amanda almost choked on that last statement.

Janice squinted through the cigarette smoke, looking them up and down. "No, you're not."

"No," Teresa said, "we're not. We work for a company that tracks down missing heirs, and we have some money for Ronald Collins."

"Brilliant!" Charley declared. Amanda had to agree.

Janice snorted. "Ronnie hasn't got any kinfolks with money."

"It's not a close relative," Amanda said before Janice could turn away.

"Very distant relative," Teresa confirmed.

"Wendell Collins who lived in Pennsylvania." The fiction sprang to her mind and from there to her lips without hesitation. The lie was necessary in order to find Collins. It had nothing to do with Charley's influence. "His branch of the family moved up there in 1934, long before Ronald was born, so he'd have no way of knowing them."

Teresa nodded. "Wendell Collins never married and never had any children."

"And he died intestate." Throwing around a few legal terms couldn't hurt. "No lineal descendants. The whole estate will be divided among any living blood relatives we can find on a *per stirpes* basis."

The baby burped down the front of his stained shirt. It was a fitting comment on Amanda's outrageous story.

"Holly, can you come take this kid?" Janice called over her shoulder.

A much younger version of the woman appeared and took the baby.

Janice wiped her arm on her T-shirt. "What about Ronnie's brother? Does he get anything?"

"Yes, his brother too," Teresa said. "But don't worry. It's a huge estate. Plenty to go around."

Janice took the cigarette from her lips and blew out a long stream of smoke then burst into raucous laughter that ended in a coughing fit.

Amanda bit her tongue to keep from telling the woman she should give up smoking.

When she stopped coughing, she shook her head and grinned wryly. "Ronnie hasn't got a brother. What do you women really want? You don't look like the trash he usually cheats with, so I'm guessing he's in some kind of trouble." She dropped the cigarette butt on the vinyl floor and crushed it with the toe of her sandal then looked up, her eyes hard. "Again."

Damn. This wasn't working out the way Amanda had planned. "We just need to verify that he lives here. We're sort of like unofficial census takers."

The woman's eyes narrowed. "My landlord send you? You tell that asshole I don't have anybody living here but me and my three kids. Yeah, I let Ronnie stay for a while, but I kicked his sorry butt out two weeks ago."

"Good for you," Teresa said. "I left my husband's sorry butt."

Smart move. Establish a connection with the woman.

"We're not from your landlord," Amanda assured her. "I need to talk to Collins. He's been harassing me." If Janice really was angry with him, she was more likely to talk to someone who was also angry with him. "He and my deceased ex-husband had some dealings, and he's coming after me to settle an old debt of my ex-husband."

"Current husband," Charley corrected.

Janice shook her head, pulled a crumpled package of cigarettes from her pocket and thumped one out. "I still don't know where he is."

"You mentioned the trashy women he hangs out with," Teresa said. "Do you think he's shacking up with one of them?"

The woman shrugged. "Probably."

"Any thoughts on where those women live? A part of town he goes back to? A bar where he hangs out?"

"Where does he work?" Amanda asked.

Janice laughed again and once more went into a coughing fit.

Amanda couldn't keep her mouth shut any longer. "You need to give up those cigarettes. Don't you know what they're doing to your lungs? Don't you want to be around to raise that baby?"

"Amanda," Teresa said from the side of her mouth. "Chill."

Amazingly the woman's gaze softened. "Yeah, I know. I'm gonna quit just as soon as things slow down a little. I'm working double shifts at the coffee shop, and the bills just keep coming." She put the cigarette back in the pack and returned it to her pocket. "And that business with Ronnie didn't help. Be glad you can't find him. He's bad news. Likes to hit women." She looked down and crushed the already battered cigarette butt again, shredding the tobacco and bits of filter into tiny flecks. When she lifted her eyes, they contained no trace of her former bravado. "I didn't kick him out," she said quietly. "He left. I wanted to kick him out, but I didn't have the guts. I was afraid of him. I've been on my own a long time. I know the score. I can take care of myself. But that one, he's bad news. He put me in the hospital first time I talked back to him. After that, I didn't talk back, but when he gets high, it don't matter. He just likes to hit people. Best I could do was keep my kids out of the way."

Amanda shivered. Great. The man trying to bully her into giving up her home and place of business took drugs and hit women. Last time she checked, she was a woman.

"Oh, I know he can be charming," Janice continued, "but don't let that fool you."

"We won't," Amanda assured her. *Charming?* Apparently she and Janice had different definitions of that word.

"He tells a woman what she wants to hear, but then when you let him move in, you find out what he's really like. I tell you the truth, I was happy when I found out he was cheating on me. When he said he was leaving, I had to bite my tongue to keep the smile off my face."

"Couldn't you have called the police or taken out a restraining order on him?"

Janice gave a short, bitter bark of laughter. "Oh, honey, you live in a completely different world. You really think a piece of paper or a cop thirty minutes away is going to stop somebody like Ronnie? You got any idea how many women get beat up or killed when the man's under a restraining order or while she's waiting on the cops to get there?"

"No, I guess I don't." Amanda moved her arm to her side and felt the reassuring outline of her .380.

"He's not so tough," Teresa said. "Amanda chased him down the street in her bare feet, throwing rocks at him."

Janice gave a burst of real laughter, delighted laughter, then coughed some more. "I'd like to of seen that." Her expression sobered. "Next time you see him, you go in your house and lock the door. He's mean, and he's got some really bad people after him that are even meaner than he is."

"Besides us?" Teresa asked.

Janice shook her head. "You don't have any idea about bad people."

Amanda and Teresa exchanged amused glances. Teresa had been married to a man who extorted millions of dollars from people, one of whom murdered him. Amanda had been married to a small time con artist who incurred the wrath of a megalomaniac who killed him and tried to kill Amanda. Then there was the evil trio that killed Dawson's parents and kidnapped his brother.

"We actually have had some experience with bad people," Amanda assured her.

"You and me, we probably got different ideas of bad people. Let me tell you about Ronnie."

Teresa gasped. "There's more?"

Janice nodded. "There's a lot more. He doesn't like to work. I bought him an old car and did my best, but I wasn't making enough money to support him and my kids. So he decided to sell a little meth. Only problem, he got greedy and ripped off his dealer."

Amanda shuddered. "That was the *only* problem?"

"Well, it was the worst. Now I got some dangerous people coming around, scaring my kids, trying to get information from me about Ronnie, and I'd tell them if I knew, but I don't. If them people find out Ronnie's coming around you, they'll be coming around you too." She looked both of them up and down again. "And I don't think you'll know how to protect yourself. Rocks aren't gonna scare these guys."

"I have more than rocks," Amanda assured her. Though the image of crazed drug lords in her parking lot was scarier than a crazed Ronald Collins.

Teresa opened her hand and displayed her stun gun. "This is more than a rock. Over a million volts of electricity."

Janice did not look impressed. "Whatever it is Ronnie wants, give it to him and get away. It's not worth your life."

Amanda shook her head. "He wants my home and my business. He won't get it. I'm filing a lawsuit against him."

Janice's eyes widened. "Your business? What kind of business? Is it big and open and not close to your neighbors?"

"Yeah, I guess so. It depends on what you consider close. I'm not out in the country or anything. I have a big double lot, far enough from my neighbors that people don't complain about the noise of my motorcycles."

Janice's thin lips tightened. "He said he'd found a place that would make a good meth house. Said the people he ripped off would be willing to take it in exchange for their money. Honey, he's not gonna stop at anything to get your building and give it to them people to save his own hide. If you're smart, you'll just let him have it."

Amanda lifted her chin. "He'll get my shop when Lubbock gets a foot of snow on the fourth of July. If you should happen to hear from him, you tell him I'm looking for him."

Chapter Fourteen

When Teresa pulled into Amanda's parking lot and the wind was no longer rushing past them, blowing away their words, Amanda released a long sigh of frustration. "We still don't have an address for Collins."

She stepped onto the hard surface of the parking lot. Heat swirled around her in the slight breeze and drifted up from the concrete. A mockingbird launched into a lilting tune in her bullet-riddled live oak tree. Maybe the mockingbird was just a visitor, but he was her visitor, his serenade was for her. It was her heat, her concrete, her tree. She'd painted the building, cleaned the grease spots off the floor from the former auto repair shop, pulled up the gross green carpet in the apartment to reveal hardwood floors, repaired the holes in the parking lot. After all that work, she was not going to let some cheap hood steal it from her and turn it into a meth lab.

"I think Janice knows more than she's saying," Teresa said. "She's scared of Collins."

Charley snorted. "He's just a two-bit punk. Amanda, you called his bluff. You're not afraid of him, are you?"

Amanda thought about it. She'd been afraid of Roland Kimball, Charley's murderer, the first time she met him. But Collins was, as Charley so aptly put it, *just a two-bit punk.* "No. Maybe I should be, but it's hard to be afraid of somebody after he runs away from you. Right now anger trumps fear, and I'm really angry at him."

"Me too," Charley said.

"Now that we've established where Collins isn't, want to grab some burgers and go by my place?" Teresa asked.

Amanda interpreted the *go by my place* to mean Teresa was offering to spend some time trying to get rid of Charley. She really, really wanted to go to Teresa's and get rid of Charley. But it would have to wait. "That sounds great, but I need to go in and do some work, give Dawson some relief, let him go home early. He has to pick up his little brother from school."

"Maybe later?"

Much as she wanted to say yes, some things had to take priority. "I need to be here in case Collins drops by again."

Teresa nodded. "I understand. But this time instead of throwing rocks at him, you might think about calling 911."

Amanda rolled her eyes. "My dad's a judge, remember? I know how likely it is that Collins is going to be convicted for hanging out at my garbage bin. He's been very careful so far not to leave any evidence that could land him in jail. I have no idea what he was planning to do before I interrupted him last night, but all he did was play in my trash."

"He may have been looking for envelopes and bills so he could steal your identity," Teresa suggested.

Amanda shook her head. "After being married to Charley, it's not like I have an identity worth stealing."

For once, Charley had nothing to say.

"How about I get my crystals and cards and bring them to your place? It might even be easier to help Charley since this is sort of his home base."

"Okay, sure. But be warned, my apartment isn't as tidy as yours."

Charley frowned. "No, it's not. You wouldn't feel comfortable there, Teresa."

"Sure I will," she replied airily. "I'll go by my place then pick up some burgers and rings and meet you back here in a couple of hours."

Teresa started her car. Amanda turned toward the shop.

"Oh, one more thing," Teresa called after her. "I'm bringing my sleeping bag and spending the night. You may need help if Ronald Collins shows up."

"No, I can handle it!" But Amanda's protest was lost in the roar of Teresa's engine as she pulled out of the parking lot. Amanda shook her head and walked toward the shop. "Not bad enough I've got a ghost who won't listen to me. Now I've got a friend who won't either."

"Yeah, I think that was pretty rude of her, inviting herself over like that. You should call her and tell her not to come."

"Ha! You liked her well enough until she started talking about helping you move on. Now you think she's being rude." Amanda paused at the door of the shop. "Get over it." She opened the door and walked in.

Dawson looked up from where he sat on the floor, working on a colorful design on a fuel tank. "How'd it go?"

Charley darted past her. "Be sure and tell him how your boyfriend hugged you and whispered in your ear."

Doing her best to ignore Charley, Amanda told Dawson about the events of the day.

Dawson shook his head. "I don't like the sound of that. Why don't you stay at my place until this blows over? Grant can move in with me, and you can have his room."

"Thanks, but if I do that, who'll be here to chase Collins off the next time he tries something? I'm not going to run from that creep."

The shop phone rang.

"That's probably Detective Daggett. He called a little while ago. Said he couldn't reach you on your cell."

Charley folded his arms. "Well, isn't that sweet? He must be worried about you."

Amanda went into the office and answered the phone. Charley was right beside her.

"Amanda, it's Jake."

"*Amanda, it's Jake*," Charley mimicked.

Amanda turned her head and moved away in an effort to avoid Charley. "Hi," she said. "What's up?"

"I was getting concerned. I called your cell phone several times, and it always went to voice mail."

Charley pressed his head through the phone. Again Amanda turned away and again he moved with

190

her. Though she knew the effort was futile, she tried to shove him away. Her hand passed through his chest.

"Amanda?" Jake asked.

"Oh, uh, yeah, sorry. What were we talking about? My cell phone. Teresa drives as fast as I do, and in a convertible, you can't hear anything over the noise of the wind. Then I left it in the car when we went up to talk to Ronald Collins' girlfriend."

"Who?"

Damn! Dealing with Charley had distracted her to the point she'd said something she hadn't intended to say. She sighed and told Jake about Collins. "So now I'm trying to find him so Sunny can have him served."

Jake was silent for a long moment. "This man threatened you, shot your tree, burned your truck, and you caught him looking through your trash. Did it ever occur to you to call the police?"

"Yeah, why didn't you just call him, let him take care of you?" Charley sniped.

"No," Amanda said, again trying to turn away from Charley. "What could you—they do? There wasn't any evidence."

"Really? You've seen what Ross can come up with even when there's no sign of any evidence."

A chill darted through Amanda's head as Charley pressed closer. "So now Ross is a magician who can produce evidence out of thin air?" Charley asked. "I don't think so."

"Okay," Amanda said, "maybe I should have called." It was difficult to focus on what Jake was saying when Charley was in her face. Literally.

"I'll come by tomorrow and take a report." He paused. "I could come by tonight and watch your place."

"Sure he could," Charley said. "Watch it from your bedroom? I hope you can see what he's trying to do, Amanda."

Amanda could only see one thing…that Charley was becoming more annoying by the second.

"That's not necessary," she assured Jake. "Teresa's coming over to spend the night."

"And bringing her toy? You have to be within arm's reach of somebody to use that thing."

"I've got a .38 revolver in my nightstand as well as the little Colt Mustang I had last night. I don't have to be very close to hurt somebody with either of those." She twisted around but Charley had no problem following her movements. It was too late in the year to wish for a tornado to come along and blow him away. Probably wouldn't work anyway considering the ease with which he'd remained perched on Teresa's convertible during their high-speed drives.

"Hang on a minute," Jake said. "I want to check something."

A click and an echoing silence told her she was on hold. She took the opportunity to turn to Charley. "I am going to kill you if you don't stop that! Oh, I can't kill you because Kimball beat me to it, but I can have Teresa send you to the middle of an iceberg in the Arctic Ocean. You'll never get to smell fajitas again, much less taste them."

"What do you want me to do? Just step aside while another man takes my wife?"

"I AM NOT YOUR WIFE!"

"Hello?"

In her fury, Amanda had not heard the click of Jake returning to the phone. "Hi, yes, I'm here."

"*Hi, yes, I'm here,*" Charley mimicked.

"Who were you talking to?"

"Nobody. Myself."

"You told yourself you're not your wife?"

"Yeah, uh, it's therapy. Since Charley was killed before our divorce was finalized, I sometimes reassure myself that we're not married, that he's not coming back."

"Fine," Charley snapped. "I'll leave and I won't come back." He vanished through the far wall of the building.

Unfortunately, she knew he couldn't or wouldn't go far.

"I just did a quick check on Ronald Collins. There are a couple of men with that name in the system. The one you described has been arrested for everything from drunk driving to murdering a man in a bar fight."

"I know. Everything but kidnapping and arson."

"And you know that...how?"

"Dawson checked him out on the Internet."

"So you know the man's violent, but you don't want a trained police officer guarding your house tonight?"

Good grief. Men and their egos. "I don't want you to have to stay up all night after you've worked all day.

Really, I'll be fine. But if Collins shows up tonight, he won't be."

"You do realize you can't shoot him unless you feel your life is in danger."

"I don't expect to have to shoot him. I'll put a pile of rocks beside my bed. You and Janice Horne may think he's a scary dude, but I'm not worried."

"And that worries me."

"Okay, it's time to leave this subject. You couldn't have called me to harass me about Collins since you didn't even know about him until after you called. Any luck finding Eduardo?"

"Maybe. We have a couple of theories. But that's not why I called."

Amanda hoped and feared he was calling to confirm their Saturday night date. If Teresa didn't do something with Charley tonight, that date could be a FEMA-sized disaster.

"How about Mexican food for dinner tomorrow night?"

"Sounds good. I love Mexican food." Charley had been there the last time she'd eaten Mexican food, and Teresa had given him his own margarita. Somehow she was going to prevent him from coming along with Jake and her.

"Pick you up about six?"

"Sure. One more thing."

"Okay."

"What did you find out about Eduardo?"

"You know I can't tell you that."

"So this is a one-sided deal? I tell you everything I find out, even give you evidence that rightfully belongs to Teresa…and, by the way, she's not very happy about that…but you won't tell me anything?"

"That pretty much sums it up."

Amanda clenched her lips. She wasn't going to get into an argument with Jake. This was the first chance they'd had…and might ever have…to talk in private. She wasn't going to ruin it by being snippy.

"That pretty much sucks." The words slipped out in spite of her good intentions.

"Yeah, I guess it does. Okay, I can tell you this much. We're pretty sure Eduardo's dead."

"That's no surprise. Teresa told you that already. Have you found his body?"

"Maybe."

Maybe? "Is this related to Anthony's murder?"

"At the moment, all we have is a theory. I may have some answers I can talk about tomorrow evening if Ross gets his tests finished by then."

That sounded promising. "Is Teresa still a suspect?"

"She's a person of interest."

"Suspect, person of interest, whatever."

"Tomorrow at six."

Amanda smiled as she hung up the phone. True, she was a little miffed at Jake because he was withholding information, but she was excited about seeing him in a non-murder related setting. And Charley was still missing. Maybe he'd stay gone for a few days. Maybe she and Jake would be able to get together without him. Maybe he had decided to cut her some slack. Maybe he had even moved on.

She turned to go to the main area of the shop. Charley stood just outside the office door, arms folded, a scowl on his face. Without a word, he turned his back to her.

Sulking? It was something he'd done in life when he didn't get his way. If she was lucky, he might decide not to speak to her for a day or two.

"Dawson, go home. Tell Grant I said *hi*."

"In a minute. I just need to finish what I'm working on." He didn't look up from his work on the shiny red gas tank but continued to move a thin paint brush along the curve, deftly adding a swirl of silver.

The smell of the paint, Dawson's intent form, the motorcycle parts strewn about in glorious disarray…the elements of her shop embraced her. *Her* shop.

Amanda's anger with Charley blended into her anger with Collins, and she was no longer just angry. She was furious. Ready to hurt somebody. Eager to hurt somebody. Since she couldn't think of anything she could do to Charley, that left Collins to bear the brunt of all her anger.

She walked to a window and looked out at her bullet-riddled tree. It had been sweet of Jake to offer to watch over her during the night, protect her from Ronald Collins. Sweet, but unnecessary. The question of the moment was, who would protect Ronald Collins from her?

Chapter Fifteen

Teresa strode through the door an hour later, a large Whataburger sack in one hand and a bulging tote bag in the other. "What are you doing in the corner, Charley?"

Amanda put down the clutch plates she was working on and stood. "He's sulking. I'm going to dinner with Jake tomorrow night, and he's not happy about it." She looked at Charley who stood with his arms crossed and a scowl on his face, hovering several inches above the floor. Had his anger propelled him upward? Maybe he'd eventually go through the ceiling and drift into space. "He hasn't said a word in almost an hour. I had no idea sulking could be such a positive experience."

Teresa smiled at Charley and lifted the Whataburger bag. "I brought three burgers and three orders of onion rings."

Charley glided to her side. "Thank you, Teresa. *You've* always been nice to me."

Amanda ignored the implied accusation. When Teresa renewed her attempts to send him into the light, he'd change his tune. "Well, the sulking was great while it lasted. Let's go upstairs and eat. That smells wonderful. I love Whataburgers."

"Who doesn't?"

They climbed the steps to Amanda's apartment and Teresa carried the Whataburger sack and her tote bag to the kitchen. She set the food on the table and the other bag in the far corner of the room. Amanda assumed it contained her crystals, candles and whatever else she needed for Charley's ticket to forever-land, but she didn't verbalize her thoughts. Charley was being reasonably pleasant at the moment. She didn't want to set him off again.

She took down two plates, sighed and added a third. Teresa had brought food for him. She'd have to give him a plate. And a Coke. She set three Cokes on the table and opened two of them. When he feigned an attempt to pull the tab, she gave in and opened his too. It seemed a shame to waste a perfectly good Coke, but what was the loss of one Coke compared to a peaceful meal?

The three of them sat at the table. She and Teresa ate the burgers and rings while Charley moved his hands and occasionally his face through his food and drink. Amanda tried not to look at him. Her mother had never liked him. She could only imagine what Beverly Caulfield would say if she could see him with his face buried in a bag of onion rings.

"This was a good choice, Teresa," he said. "I haven't had Whataburger since…well, you know."

"Since you died." Teresa spoke matter-of-factly. She took a sip of Coke then looked directly at him. "I'm sorry, but you have to accept it. It's not a bad thing. We'll all get there someday, free of the restraints of our bodies, able to focus on spiritual matters."

Charley looked toward the bag in the corner. "You brought your stuff, didn't you?"

"Yes, I did. Don't you want to move into the light, see your grandparents and the dog you had when you were a little boy?"

She got Charley's attention with the dog thing. Charley's mother had told Amanda about Barney, the half-collie he'd had when he was in grade school, but Teresa had no way to know about it. Was she taking another educated guess or had she been talking to the dog?

"Barney," Teresa said. "That's his name, isn't it?"

A spectrum of emotions played across Charley's face, but he finally settled on stubborn. "I want to stay right here with Amanda."

"What if Amanda wants you to move on to a better world?"

Charley snorted. "I know why she wants to get rid of me. She wants to get it on with that damned Detective Daggett. Well, I'm not going anywhere."

One onion ring remained on Amanda's plate, but she'd lost her appetite. "Can we make him go even if he doesn't want to?"

Teresa shrugged. "I don't know. Usually if a spirit is stranded on this side, he's eager to move on. I think I need the spirit's cooperation."

Charley leaned back in his chair, folded his arms and smiled smugly. "The spirit wants to stay right here."

Amanda slammed her empty Coke can onto the table. "This is just wrong! If you hadn't got yourself murdered, we'd be divorced and you'd have to leave me alone."

"No, I wouldn't."

Amanda picked up the empty can and hurled it at Charley. It passed through his head and landed on the floor behind the chair, dribbling sticky drops on the white vinyl. All she'd accomplished was to make a mess she'd have to clean up.

She stood and leaned toward him. "I am going to freeze you and break you into a million pieces! I'm going to suck you into a vacuum cleaner bag and toss you into a volcano! I'm going to..." It was hard to think of ways to get rid of a ghost. In the old days she'd been able to threaten to cut off his manhood with a rusty, serrated knife and stuff it in the garbage disposal or wrap him in a shower curtain and beat him to death with a hammer. Though she'd still like to do those things, they were no longer possible.

Charley sat straighter. "You can't do that. Your vacuum cleaner's bagless."

Amanda snatched up her plate but resisted the urge to throw it at him. It would only mean a bigger mess for her to clean. She picked up Charley's full plate and took them both to the sink.

"Hey, I wasn't through with that," Charley protested.

Amanda turned back to the table. "Teresa, you've got to try. Please."

Teresa drew in a deep breath and nodded. "Okay."

Charley's eyes widened. "What? You're going to run me off like a stray dog?"

"I'd never run off a stray dog," Amanda assured him. "You know how much I love animals."

"Charley," Teresa said, "people are waiting for you on the other side. Barney's waiting for you. You're upsetting the entire balance of the universe by being here when you should be on the other side." She waved a hand through the air. "You could cause earthquakes and floods and tornadoes."

"Could not." But he looked uncertain.

Teresa took her plate to the sink. "I'm going to set out my crystals and candles, and we'll all just relax for a while. How does that sound, Charley?"

"Okay, I guess. But don't try anything funny."

"Amanda, could you help me move these things to the table?"

Amanda went to the corner where Teresa's bag rested. "Did you make that up, about the floods and earthquakes?" she whispered.

"Of course. Spirits come and go to the earthly plane all the time. But he seems to need some incentive. Here, take these."

Amanda accepted three white candles and peered into the bag. "What's that? Some kind of ceremonial robe?"

"No, that's my nightgown. I told you, I'm spending the night. Okay, I didn't bring my sleeping bag, but I'll fit just fine on your sofa."

"Really, that isn't necessary." Amanda carried the candles to the table and set them down. "I appreciate the thought. Jake offered to spend the night watching, and I turned him down too."

"*Jake offered to spend the night*," Charley mimicked. "Wasn't that sweet?"

Amanda's jaw clenched, but she refused to get caught up in Charley's nonsense. There was no point in wasting her breath arguing with him. "I already ran Collins off once with a few rocks. He's a bully who runs when somebody stands up to him. Besides, I promise to sleep with a gun on my nightstand."

Teresa arranged crystals of various sizes and colors on the kitchen table. "I understand. I have no doubt you are more than a match for Ronald Collins. But you never came to slumber parties when we were in high school, so we're going to make up for that lack in your life. We're going to have a slumber party here tonight, just the three of us."

Amanda felt pleased at her new friend's efforts however silly they were. "That's very nice. But I don't think two women and a ghost constitute a slumber party."

"I could always call somebody else, maybe Jody Gordon or Patricia Dewitt."

Amanda laughed, thinking of the two girls in their class who made it into the *in crowd* not by their dazzling personalities but because everybody was afraid of them. "I think I'll pass on that." She smiled. "Okay, fine. You can spend the night and we'll have popcorn and make random phone calls to ask people if their refrigerator is running."

"We could do that. Or we could have popcorn and not make random phone calls. Besides, I confess I have an ulterior motive. Of course my primary motive is to help you, but it occurred to me when I was at home getting my things together that I might be able to lure Anthony here tonight. Maybe he and Charley can have a chat."

Great. Amanda wanted to get rid of the one ghost she already had. Now Teresa was planning to invite another one.

"Do you have room for me to put my car in your shop?" Teresa continued. "I don't like the idea of leaving it out where Cuckoo Collins can get to it."

"Oh, sure. Good idea. Let's go down and I'll open the bay door. You can park next to my motorcycles." She grabbed her keys off the counter. "Let's do it right now before it gets dark and Collins has a chance to get here and start trouble."

"I'll keep a lookout so he doesn't sneak up on you," Charley said.

He'd never been able to stay mad for long. At one time she'd liked that trait.

When Teresa's convertible was stashed safely behind a locked door, they returned to the kitchen and Charley returned to frowning and standing in the corner.

Teresa added two decks of Tarot cards to the objects on the table, sat down and spread them out. She extended a hand to Charley. "Come sit with us. We're just going to relax. I can't make you do anything you don't want to do. Amanda, maybe we should have some wine."

Amanda was pretty sure it wouldn't be possible to get Charley drunk, but there was no harm in trying. She found a bottle of red wine and poured some into three wine glasses, none of which matched.

Teresa lifted hers. "Crystal. Nice."

"They're really cheap at garage sales when the people have broken all but one or two from a set. I like variety."

Teresa produced a small box of matches and lit the candles. "I always use matches. The flame is more natural than the flame from a lighter."

Evening shadows were slipping across the windows, and the candles provided a soothing effect, an oasis of brightness in the twilight room.

"Let's each choose a card to represent us. Amanda, I think the Queen of Swords for you." She laid a large, colorful card in front of Amanda. The card depicted a queen holding a sword.

"Yeah, I like that," Amanda said.

"A strong woman with a hidden emotional side. Charley, I think the King of Wands for you." She laid a card in front of him.

"Hey, how come Amanda gets a real sword and I only get a stick?"

"It's symbolic. The stick is from nature. You're a natural leader and adventurer. And I'll take the High Priestess." She selected a card and placed it in front of her. "Now, which of my crystals do you think is the prettiest, Amanda?" Teresa's voice dropped a couple of octaves and became soft and soothing.

"That one. I like purple."

"Amethyst. The gem of fire and passion that also soothes and guards against insomnia. A stone of contradictions. Appropriate for you." Teresa handed it to her. "Hold it in your hand. Feel the warmth."

Amanda accepted the purple crystal. The edges were smooth but it didn't feel warm. However, she wasn't going to do anything to discredit Teresa's performance. "Nice," she said.

"Charley, how about you? Which of these stones is your favorite? Which calls to you? Which would you like to touch?"

Charley looked across the room and shrugged. "I don't know. They're just rocks."

"How about this blue one? It's almost the same color as your eyes." She picked up the stone and moved it close to him. "It's calcite. Very calming. Blue is the color of trust, spiritual cleansing, immortality."

Charley shrugged again.

"It's pretty, isn't it? Soothing. Go ahead and touch it."

Charley hesitantly reached one hand toward the stone, moving as if unsure but compelled. That was a good sign. Maybe Teresa could compel him right out of Amanda's life.

"How does it feel?" she asked. "Smooth? Warm?"

Charley nodded slowly. Amanda was pretty sure he couldn't feel anything, but it boded well that Teresa made him believe he could.

"Aren't you glad we have these candles? It's getting dark, but we have light, three lights, three flames flickering in the darkness, one for each of us. Do you like your candle, Charley?" Her gaze focused on him, and the flames from the candles reflected and danced in her dark eyes.

Again he nodded, the movement slow and halting, then he made a sound as if clearing his throat. "It's okay. It's just a candle."

"You could say that. It's a cylinder of wax with a wick running through the middle. Nothing unusual there. But the flame is unique. Every flame is unique. It flickers in a way that's continually changing and creating new patterns that come and go and are never the same. It's one flame, the same flame, but it's always shifting, taking new forms."

"I know what you're trying to do." Charley's voice was quiet, his words slow. "It won't work."

"I'm trying to get you to relax, to consider the light, to feel the freedom of the light."

"I don't trust you." His words were slightly slurred and seemed to come to Amanda's ears from a great distance.

"You don't have to trust me. Trust yourself. Relax and watch the flickering flame. You haven't relaxed in a long time. It's hard to be outside with the sunshine all around you but you can't feel it. You can see fajitas, but you can't taste them. Would you like to sip that glass of wine? Look at the way the flame dances and sparkles in the wine glass. The light is free. It moves and flickers from the candle to the wine, back and forth, ever changing, the same but new, free and unconfined."

The darkness of the room flowed around them, touching and cooling the back of Amanda's arms and neck while the warmth of the candle flames drifted to her face. She felt as if she were floating, her body free to dance with the fire.

"It won't work!" Charley shot up from his chair.

Amanda jumped, startled out of her concentration. Maybe it hadn't worked for Charley, but it had almost worked for her.

Teresa lifted an imploring hand. "Charley—"

"No. I don't want to do this anymore." He stood next to the light switch and ran his hands through the wall as if reaching for the wiring. Something snapped, and every light in the apartment came on. Sound exploded from the television and pictures flickered as the channels switched from one to another. "Blow out those stupid candles and let's watch a movie."

Teresa looked at Amanda and mouthed the words, *I'm sorry.* She carefully blew out all the candles.

Amanda's heart sank to the bottom of her toes. Teresa was good enough that she'd fallen into a trance, but Charley was awake and adamant that he wasn't going anywhere. Her date with Jake was less than twenty-four hours away. It didn't look good for the two of them.

"Turn that television down!" she ordered. The level of sound diminished. She looked at Teresa. "Try again, please. What if we have different cards? More candles. White wine instead of red."

"No." Charley folded his arms across his chest and stuck out his lower lip like a small child. "I'm not sitting in that chair and I'm not looking at any stupid candle flame. You try that again and I'll turn the television up so loud I won't be able to hear anything you say."

Teresa spread her hands in a gesture of helplessness. "Maybe another time."

Charley put his hands over his ears. "I can't hear you!"

Amanda clenched her hands into fists. "How about an exorcism?"

Teresa smiled tentatively as if unsure whether Amanda was joking or not. Amanda wasn't sure either. "I don't know how to do that."

She flopped onto the sofa and picked up the remote. "Let's find a comedy. I need to laugh."

"I'll make popcorn," Teresa said.

Charley took a seat in the middle of the sofa. "I love popcorn."

The movie was funny, but Amanda didn't laugh. Her brain kept conjuring images of her, Jake and Charley sitting in a restaurant, Charley standing on Jake's head, running his hands through their tacos and enchiladas, chilling their food before they could eat it, making faces at Jake, forcing himself between them if Jake tried to kiss her.

She was relieved when the final credits ran and it was time to go to bed.

She rose and stretched. "You take the bed, Teresa. I'll sleep on the sofa."

"No, you won't. This is your home, your bed, and I'm the guest." Teresa went to her bag and retrieved the white gown.

"Yeah, and I'm the hostess so I'm the boss. Besides, if you stay out here, you'll be on the front line, the first one to encounter Collins. I'm the one with the grudge against him, and I'm the one with the gun."

"This is silly," Charley said. "You're both skinny. There's plenty of room for both of you in the bed. Amanda snores, but not very loud."

"I do not, but that's probably a good idea," Amanda agreed. "I only sleep on one side, so the sheets are clean on the other."

"That used to be my side," Charley said. "But she won't let me sleep there now."

"You don't sleep," Amanda pointed out.

"I could lie between the two of you and pretend to sleep."

"No," Amanda and Teresa said at the same time.

Amanda kept watch while Teresa went into the bathroom and changed into her gown, then Teresa entertained Charley while Amanda changed.

When she came out, Teresa was already in bed with the sheet tucked under her arms. "What do you do when you're here alone and want to change clothes or take a shower?"

Amanda sank onto her side of the bed and looked at Charley. "I have to take his word that he's not watching."

"Do you ever cheat, Charley?" Teresa asked. "Do you ever look when you're not supposed to?"

Charley opened his mouth then closed it. His lips twisted and turned as if struggling.

"He's trying to tell a lie," Amanda explained.

"I'm going to go in the living room and keep watch." He disappeared through the wall.

Amanda took her .38 revolver from the nightstand drawer and set it on top then switched off the lamp and lay back on her pillow.

"That's very interesting," Teresa said, "what Charley just did. I never thought about spirits telling a lie or even trying to. That seems so unspiritual, so earthly."

"Charley tries, but he can't. He always makes that kind of face, like the words are fighting to get past his lips, but something won't let them."

"Which means Anthony may be telling me the truth and somehow I've got to get back that damned passport and flash drive and give them away."

"And the money."

She sighed. "And the money. Right now I can't see any way I'm going to get any of those items back, which means I'm going to be in your situation...haunted with visits from an ex-husband who's stuck between worlds."

Amanda laughed. "I'm going to bet this conversation has little in common with the conversations from all those slumber parties and sleep overs you went to in high school."

Teresa giggled. "We talked about living boys and teachers, never ghosts. I certainly never told anybody about Mr. Finfrock or my grandmother. They already thought I was a little strange. That would have cinched it."

"The only person I told about Charley is Sunny, my birth mother. She didn't believe me at first. I think she does now. We haven't really had a chance to talk about it since."

Teresa lifted herself on one elbow. "*Your birth mother*? You were adopted?"

"Well, sort of. It's a long story. One night when this is all over and we have a couple of glasses of wine, I'll tell you."

Reluctantly Teresa lay back down. "Okay. But I can't wait to hear this story. *Adopted?* I can't imagine your mother adopting a child to satisfy her motherly instincts. I never really knew her, of course, but she always seemed kind of aloof and rigid."

"My mother has unexpected depths. Both of my mothers." Amanda was surprised that she felt comfortable talking about Sunny to Teresa. Sharing a ghost experience with someone did establish a certain level of intimacy. In spite of the circumstances, it had been kind of a fun evening. "Good night."

"If we have a good night and no visitors, I'm actually going to be a little disappointed."

"Me too," Amanda admitted. "I'm ready to confront Collins and get this over with."

"And I'm ready to find out who killed Anthony so I can send him a thank you card and offer to appear as a character witness at his trial. Maybe then Anthony will go away and I won't have to deal with getting that passport and flash drive back."

"So really we'll only have a good night if a ghost and a psycho come to visit."

"You're right. This isn't at all like the slumber parties in high school. It's way more fun."

Chapter Sixteen

"Amanda! Wake up! He's here!"

Amanda sat bolt upright in bed. "Who? Where?"

"What's going on?" Teresa's voice was muffled with sleep.

Charley darted through the bedroom wall then back again, wringing his hands. "Ronald Collins is here! He's in the living room!"

Amanda's heart rate shifted into overdrive. Her mouth went dry. The man was there, inside her home. She picked up the gun from her nightstand. Her heart pounded all the way to her fingertips as they clutched the cold metal. She wasn't sure if she was more frightened or angry, but she knew for sure she wasn't going to let that disgusting man get away with invading her home.

"He's heading for the bedroom!" Charley disappeared through the wall then came back again. "Shoot him! Quick! Through the door! Right here!" He held a hand about four feet off the floor. "Gut shot! Now! Shoot him! Amanda!"

Trying to shut out the sounds of Charley shouting and of her own heart pounding in her ears, Amanda stood and pressed back as close as she could to the bed. She wanted to stay in the shadows until Collins came in and she could get between him and the door to trap him in the bedroom. If he saw her and tried to run, she couldn't shoot him in the back. Well, she could, but Jake would frown on it. That would probably be even more of a relationship killer than taking Charley along on their first date.

She cocked the hammer and took her stance, waiting.

"He's almost here!" Charley lifted his hand higher. "Head shot! You can do it!"

She would really like for Charley to shut up just once, but he wasn't going to.

Teresa came quietly around the bed.

In the excitement, Amanda had forgotten about her guest. "Get behind me," she whispered.

"No." Teresa slipped silently to the other side of the door. The moonlight coming through the window glowed on her white nightgown, making her look as ghostly as Charley. Amanda's dark red nightshirt would, she hoped, let her stay hidden until he got into the room.

The door began to open slowly.

"Shoot!" Charley shouted again. "What are you waiting for?"

Amanda stiffened, ordered herself to relax, to focus on the gun sight, to hold her finger steady on the trigger.

A hinge creaked and the door stopped moving.

Amanda held her breath.

The door moved again.

"Shoot him!"

Perspiration gathered on her forehead. Charley's antics were as much the cause of that perspiration as

Collins' presence. She wanted to scream at Charley to shut up, but she didn't dare. She didn't want to scare Collins away, let him have time to regroup and come back another time. This needed to end tonight.

The door slid quietly open and a tall figure with a beard and baseball cap took one step into the room then stopped, looking around.

Damn! Amanda needed him to come farther in.

His head turned toward the bed, toward her, and his eyes widened.

"Don't move!" she ordered. "I'd like nothing better than to blow your bald head right off your neck and kick it down the stairs."

The man froze then turned as if to run.

"Stop!" But he wouldn't, and she didn't dare shoot him in the back.

Before he could get through the doorway, Teresa appeared behind him and lifted a hand to his neck. Electricity sizzled through the air and around the man's throat. Slowly he crumpled to the floor.

"I got him!" Teresa brandished her stun gun. "Quick! Call the cops. He won't be out forever unless he had a bad heart and I killed him." She didn't sound even a little remorseful at that possibility.

Amanda had thought about killing him, but the idea of actually having a dead body in her bedroom was a little creepy. She released the hammer and set her gun on the nightstand. "You think he's dead?"

Teresa looked all around the room then shook her head. "No. I don't see his spirit. He's alive."

It was a better method than touching his neck to feel for a pulse and maybe getting lice from that beard.

Amanda laid down her gun, picked up her cell phone and dialed 911. "I have an intruder." She gave her name and address then hung up before the woman could ask for more information. She wasn't sure how much time she'd have before the cops got there, and she wanted to spend that time waking Collins and having a heart to heart chat with him.

She flipped on the lamp and strode over to where the man lay. With one foot she turned him over.

The baseball cap came off exposing a full head of hair.

"That's not Ronnie," Charley said.

"What? Sure it's him. So he got a hairpiece. I saw him wearing this cap the night we went out for Mexican food. It's Collins. Look at that ratty beard."

Teresa frowned and held the stun gun toward Amanda. "Take this."

Amanda accepted the object and set it behind her on the night stand. "What's wrong?"

Teresa leaned slowly toward the body. "This is not possible." Her words were muffled as if she pulled them from the depths of her being.

Had Teresa accidentally zapped herself with her stun gun?

"Don't get too close," Amanda warned.

Teresa reached down, grabbed the beard and tugged. It came off in her hand. She gasped, tossed the beard across the room, and stepped backward, her eyes wide and her face pale. Her mouth opened but no sound came out.

"Are you all right?"

Teresa closed her mouth, swallowed, looked at Amanda then at Charley then back to the man on the floor. "That's Anthony." Her voice was quiet and strained. "That's my ex-husband."

Teresa must have zapped herself and it had affected her brain. Amanda leaned over and tentatively touched the man's shoulder. It was real and solid. "This is not your ex. Your ex is dead, and this isn't a ghost." But this man did look a lot like the pictures Amanda had seen of Anthony. Still, it was a generic look…Italian, Greek, Hispanic.

Teresa looked down again and shivered. "I know he's dead, and this can't be him, but it is. I swear it's him. I don't understand."

Neither did Amanda. Obviously the man who'd broken into her apartment wasn't Ronald Collins, but it didn't look like a ghost either. Unless some ghosts were more material than others. "You did say you wanted to try to lure Anthony here tonight to talk to Charley."

Teresa's eyes widened and she gazed at Amanda in horror. "Oh no. I'm so sorry. I told his ghost—I mean, him—that you have the flash drive and passport. He came to get it. Damn! It's him, all right. He's not dead. Now I suppose I'll have to start the divorce proceedings all over again and pay more lawyers' fees!" She gave the body a savage kick.

"Teresa, Anthony's dead. They found Anthony's body in the garage."

"Burned beyond recognition."

Amanda's gaze met Teresa's as the implications of that detail sank in.

In the dead silence that followed, Amanda heard the distinct clicking sound of her front door knob turning.

She froze. "The cops would knock, wouldn't they?" she said softly.

"I've got this." Charley darted past them through the living room.

Teresa pointed at the lamp. "The light."

The living room was dark, and they didn't want to be spotlighted for the benefit of whoever was breaking in now. Amanda switched the lamp off just as the front door began to slowly creak open.

Charley rushed back to them, not even bothering to move his feet in a pretense of running. "It's Collins! I'm sure this time!"

Amanda looked at the unconscious man on her bedroom floor. Apparently the local organization of home invaders was having their Friday night get-together at her home. And she was still in her nightshirt.

"Amanda! He's coming!" Charley warned.

The real Collins' appearance in her apartment seemed anti-climactic, almost an after-thought. Amanda reminded herself he was real, that a crazy man was breaking into her home. Another crazy man.

She grabbed an arm of the first intruder. "Help me move him. We need to close the bedroom door."

Charley and Teresa both grabbed the other arm. Amanda and Teresa tugged the man farther inside the room while Charley pretended to help.

Charley darted back into the living room then returned to the bedroom. "Hurry! He's got the door open enough to come in!"

Amanda eased the bedroom door almost closed and peeked out the opening.

Collins stuck his bald head and ugly beard into her living room then came in, closing the door quietly behind him.

Amanda's mouth went dry. She reached behind her and lifted her .38 from the nightstand.

Collins walked through her living room with a swagger, leaning to run a hand over the cushions of her sofa. They would have to be cleaned.

As he approached, Amanda again cocked the hammer of her revolver. The small click sounded eerily loud, seemed to echo in the darkness.

A wide smile split the scraggly beard. "I spy somebody's little eye peeking through the door. Amanda, here's Ronnie!"

Amanda swung the door wide and stepped out, leveling her gun at him. "Don't move, and don't touch anything else."

He deliberately traced his fingers over the shade of her floor lamp. "Isn't that cute? Got yourself a little gun. Charley said you was a spitfire."

Charley shrugged. "I did."

"He's right. Now get your greasy fingers off my property before I shoot you with this little gun that's loaded with .38 hollow points."

"You don't want to do that."

"Actually, I do. I really do. I've been fantasizing about it ever since the first time you stepped through my door with your shiny head and ugly beard and that stupid piece of paper that my idiot ex-husband signed when he had no right to."

Charley flinched. "You don't have to be mean about it."

Collins' grin widened. "Now you got me. What you gonna do with me?"

That was a good question. Since she was the one with the gun, Amanda didn't fear for her life. That meant she didn't have the legal right to shoot him. What did one do when holding a man at gunpoint and waiting for the police to arrive?

"Sit down on the sofa." She didn't want him sitting on her furniture, but she didn't want him leaving before the cops got there either.

"Whatever you say, sweetheart." He sank onto the sofa, the macabre smile still on his face. "You look good in that short gown. Nice legs."

"Hey!" Charley darted through the coffee table and stood in front of Collins. "You can't talk to my wife like that!"

Amanda released the hammer of her .38 but kept the gun in her hand as she moved slowly across the room. She bent to turn on a lamp then sat on the chair facing the sofa. Charley perched on the arm next to her.

She could see Teresa's outline in the shadows of the bedroom, but with the light on in the living room, Collins probably couldn't see her. He wasn't expecting anybody else to be there. Thank goodness Teresa was hanging back, not rushing out with her stun gun to save the day. Now all she had to do was keep this crazy man in her apartment until the cops arrived.

Collins draped an arm along the back of the sofa. "This is a nice place. I'm gonna like living here."

Amanda leaned forward. "What is wrong with you? You can't just come in and take my home and my business."

"Your husband gave me a piece of paper that says I can. You got anything to drink? My mouth's kind of dry."

"I have plenty to drink, but you're not getting any of it." She shook her head. "You are bat crap crazy. My attorney has already filed a lawsuit to discount that piece of paper."

Collins snorted. "You got a lot to learn about how things are done in the real world, Miss Highland Park. I got a piece of paper says I own this place, and I got the power to run you out of it no matter what some attorney with a fancy degree says."

Amanda's fingers tightened around the gun in her lap. To shoot or not to shoot. She sighed. Not really an option when he was apparently unarmed, both weapon-wise and mentally. "I've got the law and a .38 that say you're wrong on both counts." She leaned toward him. "Look, I understand you've got drug dealers coming after you, but that's not my problem."

"Yeah, I know you talked to Janice. You think I wouldn't find out? She tells me things."

Amanda frowned, remembering Janice's fear when she talked about Collins. "Yeah, she tells you things when you beat her."

"I never beat her. Sure, I hit her a few times. She likes it. Makes her feel like a real woman. Did you feel that way when Charley hit you?"

Charley turned to her, his eyes wide. "I never told him that!"

Makes her feel like a real woman? Amanda's jaw clenched. She really, really wanted to shoot the man but she wouldn't have time to hide the body before the cops arrived. "Charley never hit me. He had a lot of problems and did a lot of things wrong, but that wasn't one of them."

"Too bad. You might have liked it."

"Or I might have shot him."

Collins' grin got even wider. "You are sassy. Guess it goes with the red hair. I had me a red head once. She wasn't so sassy when I got through with her." He took a crumpled package of cigarettes from his shirt pocket, tamped one out and put it in his mouth.

As if the insults weren't bad enough, now he was going to stink up her apartment. "No smoking in my home. You light that, and you're a dead man."

He laughed, drew a lighter from his pocket and prepared to light up.

Amanda stood, strode across the room and snatched the cigarette from his mouth. "I said, *no smoking*. Are you hard of hearing or just stupid?"

Collins grabbed her wrist with one hand and pulled her so close she could smell the rotten stench of his breath. "No woman talks to me that way."

Now that she was closer, she could see the night glittering in his eyes, eyes that seemed to be completely black with no iris. Did meth cause pupil dilation? It wasn't something she'd thought about or researched. Janice had said he got more dangerous when he was on drugs. Whatever the problem was, it ramped up her levels of fear and anger.

He laughed, the sound ugly and dark, erupting from his gut through the scraggly beard.

"Amanda, I think he's high." Good old Charley. Master of the understatement.

Amanda made no attempt to free her wrist but aimed her gun at his crotch. He was restraining her. Surely that gave her the right to shoot him.

"Turn me loose." She kept her voice calm though her insides were in turmoil. Was it true that someone on meth could take a gunshot and keep coming like the monsters in horror movies? She had five rounds in her .38. Would that be enough to stop him?

His fingers tightened around her wrist and he jerked her closer. "You gonna shoot me if I don't? Is that thing even loaded?"

Charley floated up beside her. "Amanda, we got a problem." Again with the understatement.

"Don't anybody move."

Amanda's head jerked toward the bedroom, toward the sound of the new player.

The first Ronald Collins, the one with hair and no beard, held Teresa in front of him, one arm around her throat, a Glock pressed to the side of her head.

Chapter Seventeen

His attention diverted, Collins' grip around Amanda's wrist loosened and she twisted away, hiding her gun behind her back. The man could shoot Teresa before Amanda could get her weapon aimed. She had to wait for the right time.

"Who the hell are you?" Collins demanded. "What's going on here?"

"I want my property." The man's voice was firm and well-modulated as if he was accustomed to being obeyed.

Two of them in her living room. Two bullets each and one to spare.

"Your property?" she asked. "What are you talking about?"

"Yeah, this place is *my* property," Collins said.

"It's Anthony." Teresa's voice was small and choked.

Amanda shook her head. "No. You're dead. I mean, he's dead."

Collins shot up from the sofa. "Who's dead?"

"Obviously I'm not dead. I'm alive and I want my passport and that flash drive."

Teresa gave a slight shake of her head, as much as she could in her restricted position.

Amanda interpreted it as a warning not to admit she'd given the items to the cops.

Stall.

"Who the hell are you?" Collins repeated. Limited vocabulary.

"Sit down and shut up," Amanda directed. She had to focus on the situation with Anthony. Bad enough she had to deal with Charley's interference. Now she had another mouthy jerk in the room.

"Who do you think you're talking to, bitch?" Collins reached for Amanda again, but she stepped backward and he stumbled, barely righting himself before falling.

"Okay, but you have to prove you're Anthony Hocker," she said to the man holding a gun to Teresa's head. "As far as I know, you're dead. I'm not giving anything to some imposter."

Anthony's lips thinned and he jerked Teresa tighter. "Tell her who I am."

Teresa clutched at Anthony's arm with both hands and made choking noises.

He loosened his grip. "Tell her who I am."

"It's Anthony."

"Not great validation when you're choking her. You could make her say anything you want. If you're Anthony, who do the police have in the morgue?"

"Atta girl," Charley encouraged. "You're really good at frustrating people."

Amanda let that one go but saved it for later.

"Somebody's in the morgue?" Collins inched closer. "Who's in the morgue? Amanda, have you been a bad girl?"

"It's Eduardo, isn't it?" Teresa asked.

"Eduardo was the same height and body build as me, the same hair and skin. I figured nobody would miss an illegal alien."

Amanda thought of the tears in Isabel's eyes, of Eduardo's widow and fatherless children in Mexico. "Somebody misses him."

"I really don't care. I just want my passport and list of bank accounts so I can get the hell out of here."

Collins waved an arm toward the door. "Yeah, you need to get the hell out of here." He took another step closer to Hocker and Teresa.

Amanda moved into a direct path between the two. She couldn't risk Collins doing something stupid and causing Anthony to shoot Teresa.

Keep Teresa alive and stall until the cops got there. Janice's words about how many women were assaulted or killed while waiting for the police to arrive echoed through her mind.

"That was you outside the Mexican restaurant, wasn't it? I thought it was him—" Amanda jerked her head in Collins' direction— "but it was you, following Teresa. You were driving an old car."

"That clunker was all I could buy with the cash I had on hand because this bitch took my money. She's been driving around in that flashy car of hers while I drive that piece of crap." His face became even darker, the rage increasing.

Perhaps that had not been a good choice of subject for stalling. Amanda's mind went blank. She couldn't come up with any other topics of conversation. *Seen any good movies lately?* probably wouldn't work.

"I don't know who you people are, but you need to get out of here. Me and Amanda was having a nice little talk before you showed up." Collins took another step toward Anthony who pressed the gun more tightly to Teresa's head.

"Back off, baldy, or I'll shoot the bitch."

"You shut your mouth!" Collins lunged toward Teresa and Anthony.

Charley ran between them, and Amanda threw herself at Collins. They both tumbled to the floor with her on top. Collins cursed and floundered to his knees.

Amanda got to her feet but he grabbed her ankle with one hand and reached up toward her arm with the other. She had no choice. She couldn't let him put Teresa's life in jeopardy. She shoved the gun barrel against his hand and squeezed the trigger. He screamed. That was one hand that would never batter a woman again.

Apparently what they said about meth users was true. He staggered to his feet and surged toward Hocker again. Amanda shot his right knee. Surely with no knee cap he couldn't keep moving.

He screamed and fell to the floor, holding his knee, cursing and bleeding all over her hardwood floors. Thank goodness she hadn't had carpet installed.

"Put the gun down," Anthony ordered, his voice suddenly quiet. "Put the gun down *now* and get my passport and flash drive *now*. We've just run out of time. Somebody may have heard those shots."

"Call a doctor," Collins begged. "That bitch shot me!"

Amanda set her gun carefully on the coffee table and lifted her hands. "Okay, got it. Your things are in the safe downstairs in my shop. I'll go get them."

"We'll all go downstairs and get them."

"Okay. I just need my keys."

"Where are your keys?"

"In the bedroom. You think I'd leave them out here where some intruder could get them?"

"Help me!" Collins clutched his bleeding knee. Amanda resisted the urge to kick him in his wound. She was barefoot and didn't want to get his blood on her skin.

Anthony stepped out of the doorway, tugging Teresa with him. Amanda slid past him, into the bedroom. Her keys lay on the nightstand next to Teresa's toy. She laid her hand on the keys then hesitated. She'd seen how powerful that stun gun was. She slid her other hand toward it.

"Don't even think about it," Anthony ordered, and she jerked her hand back. "And you shut the hell up!" He kicked Collins in the head with a booted foot, and the meth man slumped unconscious on the floor.

Amanda was glad she didn't have to listen to him anymore, but Anthony had no right to do that. Collins was hers to hurt.

She glared at him as she moved past him. "Dickhead."

"What did you say?" he demanded.

She turned to face him. "Dick. Head."

Before he could respond, someone pounded on the front door. "Police! Open up!"

Collins moaned.

227

Anthony cursed.

Charley darted through the door then came back. "It's the cops all right. Two uniforms."

Beads of sweat broke out on Anthony's forehead.

"It's over," Amanda said. "Let her go."

"If you want your friend to live, you tell those cops to get in their car and drive away. Then we'll all go downstairs, get my passport and bank accounts, and the three of us will drive until I'm sure we're not being followed. Then you two will get out and walk while I leave the country. Otherwise, you can both die right now. I'll go to prison, but you won't be around to see it."

Amanda could see two major problems with that scenario. She could get him a copy of the numbers for his bank accounts, but she didn't have the passport. The second problem was equally insurmountable. She couldn't imagine him letting Teresa and her live when they knew the phony name on his passport and could alert authorities to that as well as his foreign bank accounts.

He pulled Teresa tighter against him, and she gave a frightened squeak. "Get rid of them," he said.

She set her keys on the coffee table, lifted her hands in a gesture of surrender and turned toward the door. "All right! Hold on, I'm coming!" She strode over and opened the door halfway. Two uniformed police officers stood there. "Hi." She tried to sound normal for Anthony's benefit, but rolled her eyes to the side to let the officers know that things weren't normal.

"We had a 911 call about an intruder at this address."

"That wasn't me." She moved her eyes up and down in a nodding motion to indicate she was negating what she'd just said.

"The caller gave the name Amanda Caulfield."

"I'm Amanda, but I didn't call. It was probably my daughter."

"You don't have a daughter," Charley protested. "They'll check and find out you don't have a daughter and then they'll know...oh, I see. Good idea!"

"She went to a slumber party tonight," Amanda continued, "and I let her take my cell phone, and you know what silly things those teenage girls can get up to." She twisted her lips and made a negative motion with one hand.

The officers exchanged dubious glances. The taller man shifted and dropped his hand to rest casually beside his gun. "We heard shots and screaming coming from your apartment."

"The shots, oh, yeah, the shots. I was cleaning my gun, and it went off."

The second officer frowned. "Twice?"

"Yeah, pretty careless of me. I'm not very familiar with guns." If they checked, they'd find she'd gone through training and had a permit to carry a concealed weapon.

"And the screaming?"

"Television. I was playing it really loud. It's quiet and lonesome around here without my daughter." She pointed her index finger with the other fingers folded, making the sign of a gun, then lifted her index finger to her chin and made a face.

"Ma'am, are you all right?" the taller officer asked.

"Oh, sure, I'm fine."

"You don't seem fine. Are you having some kind of a seizure?"

So much for her attempts to communicate. "I'm fine."

"We'd really like to come inside and talk with you."

"No! No, that wouldn't be a good idea. The place is a mess. I haven't had a chance to clean what with my daughter home for the summer." If they did even the most cursory check on her, they'd realize she had no daughter and then they'd surely understand she'd been trying to tell them she needed help, that someone was inside with a gun, that they should bring the SWAT team, call out the negotiators, bring in the hounds, take some sort of action.

"Ma'am, we don't care what your house looks like."

"Oh, there goes the oven timer. I have to get back to my cake. It's a wedding cake. I can't let it overcook."

"Good one," Charley said. "Everybody knows the only time you turned on that oven was by accident. You couldn't bake a cake if somebody else mixed it for you."

Amanda could have done without Charley's encouragement. She forced a phony smile to her lips. "Thank you so much for dropping by."

She closed the door and turned back into the room.

Nothing had changed. Collins still lay on the floor, unconscious and bleeding. Anthony still held a gun to Teresa's head. Surely his arm would get tired eventually.

Footsteps sounded going down the stairs outside. Were the officers stomping unusually loudly so Anthony would think they were leaving when they really weren't?

"Look out the window and tell me when they're gone," Anthony ordered.

Amanda went to the front window and looked out. Her heart sank as she watched the men walk across her parking lot to the street, get in their cruiser and drive away. Damn. But maybe they were only going around the block. Maybe they'd be back.

"They're gone," Charley announced. "I guess they didn't understand what you were trying to tell them."

All the facial contortions and eye rolling had done nothing except make them think she was having a seizure. She turned back to the drama in her living room. "They left."

Teresa closed her eyes and Amanda didn't have to be psychic to know what she was thinking. The cops were gone along with their best chance of rescue.

But not their only chance.

Amanda lifted her gaze to Anthony's, to the shadowed malice and greed. He had killed a man because he valued money more than that man's life. He counted the man of no consequence. He counted the woman he'd married of no consequence, and that woman was Amanda's friend.

Amanda would come up with something.

"Let's go." Anthony waved the gun toward the door.

Amanda opened the door and stepped outside. Dark and silent. The street light was still out. The sliver of moon shed little light on the area, and the bar down the street was closed, its neon signs dark.

She started down the stairs.

No one walking down the street. No cop cars driving back around the block. She was on her own.

Charley appeared beside her. "I think Ronnie's waking up. I'll ask him to get your gun and come down and..." He sighed. "No, I won't, will I? You and Teresa are the only people who can hear me."

Really? Even if Collins could hear him and even if Collins could walk with a shattered knee cap, telling him to get a gun and come help them was about the dumbest idea Charley had ever come up with. "Tell Teresa everything's going to be okay, that I have a plan," she whispered.

"I knew you'd think of something. What are you going to do?"

"I have no idea, but tell her anyway."

"Are you talking to yourself?" Anthony demanded.

Amanda reached the bottom of the stairs and turned an angry stare on him. "Yes, I am. Do you have a problem with that?"

"I don't care what you do just as long as you get me my passport and bank accounts."

Amanda moved slowly to the shop door, buying time, hoping to think of something.

"Don't worry," she heard Charley say. "Amanda's got everything..." He choked and tried again. "Amanda..." Damn! She'd forgotten he couldn't tell a lie. "Amanda said to tell you she has a plan."

Amanda smiled. Charley was sneaky. He could even get around the celestial prohibition against lying.

She slid her key into the lock and turned it slowly.

Think! There were lots of tools and metal pieces lying around and they'd have to walk past them to get to the back room where the safe was located. Maybe she could shove something in his path and make him trip...if he wasn't holding that blasted gun to Teresa's head. If he tripped and fell, he might squeeze the trigger. That would not be a good thing.

She flipped on the light switch and moved slowly across the large open area. Thanks to Dawson, it was relatively clean and free of debris.

Think!

"Can't you walk any faster?" Anthony demanded. "Where is this safe?"

"In the office. Duh." Amanda reached the room at the back and went in, moving slowly around the desk to the small safe in the corner.

"Hurry up. Open it so we can get out of here before your cop friends come back."

"They're gone. They're not coming back." She hoped that was a lie.

She sat down in front of the safe and began twirling the dial back and forth, careful not to stop on any of the correct numbers of the combination.

Charley crouched beside her. "Go slow! I'll think of something!"

She arched a dubious eyebrow and kept twirling the dial.

"What are you doing?" Anthony demanded. "Get it open. Now!"

"Stop bullying me! You've got me so nervous, I can't remember the combination."

"You'd better remember it soon unless you want your friend's brains splattered all over this place. I know she doesn't have many, but it's still going to be quite a mess."

"Hi, Grandma Minerva!" Teresa said, her voice weak and shaky. Not surprising under the circumstances.

"Don't start with that ghost stuff," Anthony ordered. He sounded angry but just a little bit uncertain. "Your ghosts are about as real as the speaker I hid in your apartment so I could stand outside and talk to you. Only there's no speaker here. You're just nuts."

"She said for me to tell her little Tony that she's ashamed of him." Teresa sounded stronger, as if she really was talking to his grandmother. If not, she was getting into the swing of her act.

"Shut up, you crazy bitch!"

Amanda sneaked a peek up at him. The perspiration on his forehead was moving down the bridge of his nose. He was losing his cool. She wasn't sure if that was good or bad.

Charley looked around carefully. "I think maybe I kind of see his grandmother over there against the wall."

He couldn't lie so he must really believe he could *maybe kind of see* Teresa's grandmother. Amanda doubted he could actually see the spirit. She also had her doubts that Teresa could see her. Teresa was a gifted medium, but she was also a talented performer.

"She wants you to think about when you were seven and broke your dad's watch. She knew he'd beat you if he found out, so she told him she did it. Now she wants a favor from you."

"I said, shut up! And you—if you don't get that safe open now, I'm going to start putting bullets in your crazy friend here. I'll start with her knees since that worked so well on that man in your apartment."

"She wants you to face up to the wrongs you've done," Teresa continued. "She can't take your punishment for you this time."

"I told you, no more ghost crap!"

Amanda ducked her head and twirled the dial faster. "Check outside," she whispered to Charley. Surely the cops had time to decode her verbal and ocular clues and come back with a SWAT team.

"What?" he asked.

"The left knee in ten seconds," Anthony warned.

A psychotic killer and a deaf ghost. Not a good combination.

"Ten…nine…"

Amanda shot to her feet, hands in the air. "Outside! I'm going outside."

"What? No, you're not! Get that safe open now. You have eight seconds."

"My hands are sweaty. My fingers are slipping on the dial. I need to go outside." She rolled her eyes in Charley's direction and twitched her head toward the door. "*You* need to go outside."

"You want me to go outside?" Charley asked.

"And look around."

He finally got the message and left the room.

"You're as crazy as she is." Perspiration trickled down the sides of Anthony's face.

"Your grandmother says she's going to spank your little bottom—isn't that cute, that she calls it your little bottom?—if you don't straighten up and act like her good boy."

"Seven seconds."

Charley appeared through the open door. "Cops are here! That damned Daggett and Ross and two more I don't recognize. They're right outside this place but they're pointing up to your apartment. I don't think they know you're down here."

The fear in Teresa's eyes lessened slightly as she heard Charley's words.

"Six!"

Charley couldn't tell the cops where they were but he could manipulate electricity. "Blink!" Amanda shouted.

Anthony blinked...several times in rapid succession. "What? Are you on some kind of drugs?"

At least he'd stopped counting.

"Blink the lights in the shop!" At that point, what difference did one more strange comment make? She whirled around and plopped back down at the safe, spinning it rapidly to the correct combination and swinging it open to display several stacks of papers and a metal cash box.

She could see slight shifts in the light coming through the open door as Charley flashed the lights in the shop on and off repeatedly creating a strobe effect.

"It's here." She held up her own passport. She needed to divert Anthony's attention from the flashing lights and from Teresa. He wouldn't know it was the wrong passport until he looked inside. With any sort of luck, that wouldn't happen.

"Where's my flash drive?"

"In the box." Dawson kept several flash drives in the cash box, backups of various documents, diagrams and pictures. She grabbed one that looked similar to Anthony's and held it up in her other hand. "Ta da! Here they are. Now you can relax."

"Good girl. Give them to me."

Amanda stood and moved slowly toward Anthony and Teresa. From the corner of her eye she could see dark figures slipping through the strobe lights into her shop.

Anthony still held the gun pressed so tightly against Teresa's temple she would have an imprint when this was over. Or a bullet hole.

Amanda held the passport and flash drive out to Anthony. "Take them. I'm damn sure not going to stick my hand in your pocket."

"They're here!" Charley announced.

Teresa's eyes widened briefly then she closed them, moaned and slumped as if in a faint, a dead weight on Anthony's arm. The gun was no longer against her temple.

Amanda launched herself at Anthony, throwing him off balance. The gun exploded, but the bullet went through the wall, not Teresa's head.

Teresa spun and added her weight to Amanda's, sending Anthony to the floor.

"Police!"

"Help!" Amanda shouted, struggling to keep Anthony down as he squirmed.

Teresa slammed her elbow into his crotch and he shrieked. "Pretty sensitive for a dead man."

"Everybody on your feet!" Jake's rough voice came to Amanda's ears as beautiful music.

She pushed away from Anthony and stumbled to a standing position. Teresa got to her feet more slowly, giving her undead husband a final kick as she rose.

Cops with guns seemed to fill the small room though there were only four of them. Jake and Ross were front and center.

"It's Anthony Hocker," Amanda said. "He's alive."

"We know," Jake said.

"You know? How could you know?"

"I got the DNA results," Ross said. "The body wasn't his." Teresa ran to him, and he wrapped one arm around her while keeping his gun pointed at Anthony. "You're under arrest for murder. Cuff him."

The uniformed officers hauled Anthony to his feet and one slapped handcuffs on him while the other restrained him.

"You have the right to remain silent," Jake said. "Anything you say can and will be used against you in a court of law."

"I want my lawyer." Anthony glowered at Teresa. "This isn't over, bitch."

Ross held Teresa tighter against him. "Actually, it is," he said. "Take this jerk to the station, and we'll be right behind you to process him."

The officers left with Anthony in tow. Only Jake, Ross, Amanda, Teresa, and, of course, Charley remained in the small room.

Jake and Ross holstered their guns, and Ross wrapped both arms around Teresa. "Are you all right?" he asked, stroking her hair.

She snuggled against his chest and nodded. "I am now."

Amanda wanted to go to Jake the way Teresa went to Ross, to feel his arms about her, holding her up and giving her strength. She felt weak and shaky now that the danger was finally over and the adrenalin ebbing.

But Charley stood between Jake and her, watching her every movement.

"I'm glad you're safe," Jake said. "I'm glad I could help you."

She leaned against the desk and twisted her lips into a smile she hoped looked more natural than it felt. "I've never been so happy to see the cops. Kind of makes up for all the times I saw one of you in my rearview mirror and hated him because I knew he'd be giving me a speeding ticket. I was afraid those first guys who came to my apartment wouldn't get my messages."

Jake moved closer.

Charley remained between them.

"Messages?" Jake repeated. "You mean acting like you were having a seizure?"

"Isn't that why you're here?"

"Yes and no. We were working late, trying to figure out where to go with the results of that DNA."

Teresa jerked away and gaped at Ross. "You didn't think maybe you should tell me immediately?"

Ross grinned and pulled her back to him. "No, not in the middle of the night."

"I was worried about you after our talk," Jake said. "I checked the trouble reports and saw the information about your 911 call. I tried to call your cell phone and got no answer. I was worried that creep you'd told me about was bothering you."

Amanda's eyes widened and she stood upright. "Oh! I forgot all about him!"

"It's okay," Jake assured her. "I'll take care of him."

"Uh, yeah, somebody needs to. He's upstairs bleeding all over my floor."

Chapter Eighteen

The sky was getting light in the east by the time Amanda got back to bed.

Anthony Hocker was securely behind bars and Ronald Collins was in the hospital awaiting transfer to jail. Jake and Ross left with him, and Teresa went home. Bad guys out of the picture, slumber party over.

Of course Amanda had no time alone with Jake. Not that she ever did with Charley always around. She would have liked a minute or two with him, a chance to relax, to talk about the men who'd invaded her home, about how scared she'd been, how relieved she was that it was over. But that didn't happen.

She settled into bed and tugged the sheet over her. The slumber party with Teresa had been kind of fun, but the rest of the night had gone rapidly downhill. Thank goodness she no longer had to worry about Collins burning down her apartment or shooting her plant life. She could get some sleep and be ready for her date tomorrow...tonight...with Jake. And Charley.

"Good night, Charley." For a brief instant she dared to hope he wouldn't answer, that he'd be gone.

"Good night, Amanda. I hope Teresa's okay. I wish she'd stayed here."

"She's fine. Go to sleep. Or wherever it is you go."

241

༺༻

Amanda woke to the sound of her phone.

Jake.

She sat up in bed and rubbed the sleep from her eyes, trying to clear the fog from her brain. "Good morning."

"How are you doing? Did you get some rest?"

Amanda looked at the clock. "Almost six hours. How about you?" Was he going to be too tired for their date? She would be devastated...and a little relieved. She wouldn't have to deal with Charley.

"I got a couple of hours. I just wanted to see if you're going to feel up to going out tonight."

"Absolutely. If you are. I mean, if you're too tired, I understand."

"I'm not tired. But you went through a pretty traumatic experience last night."

"Yes, but that was last night. I'm fine today."

"So we're still on for six?"

"You bet. What should I wear? Dressy? Blue jeans?"

"How about dressy blue jeans?"

"Sounds like my kind of evening. See you tonight."

She disconnected the call and realized she was smiling...until she saw Charley standing next to the bed with a huge scowl on his face.

"That was disgusting," he said.

She fell back onto the bed and pulled the pillow over her head.

"That's right, hide your face in shame."

Amanda sat up in bed. "This has got to stop. Let's go get some breakfast and talk."

"I can't eat, remember? I'm just stuck here in the middle of nowhere, can't eat, can't sleep, and I'm forced to listen to my wife make a date with another man."

Amanda lifted her hands to her face and groaned.

"You need to call that man and tell him you're not going with him tonight," Charley ordered.

Maybe she should do that. She wanted to spend time with Jake, get to know him better, relax for an evening of fun. But that wasn't going to happen with Charley around.

She vaulted out of bed, fisted her hands on her hips and faced him. "No. This is all so wrong. You're dead. We're not married anymore. We almost weren't married when you were killed. I'm sorry you're stuck in between. I'm sorry you can't eat or drink or feel the sunshine. But that's partially your fault. Teresa tried to send you on to the spiritual world, and you resisted."

He flinched and looked away. "I don't want to talk about Teresa."

"Then let's talk about me. I'm still alive. I can still eat and drink and have relationships with living people. I can get married again and make love with my husband and maybe have children. I can't do any of those things with a ghost. Be reasonable, Charley. You're violating the natural order of things."

As usual when confronted with logic he didn't like, Charley narrowed his eyes, crossed his arms and turned away.

243

Amanda glared at his back. "That's the best you've got? When you were alive, you'd have stormed out of the house and gone to a bar. Why don't you do that now? If you want to believe we're still married, act like it. Leave. Go get drunk and pick up some bimbo."

He said nothing. Maybe he was going to sulk again. That would be pleasant for as long as it lasted, but she knew it wouldn't last through her evening with Jake.

She picked up the phone to call Teresa. Maybe she could try again to get Charley on his way.

Charley whirled around and ran his hand through the phone, effectively cutting off the call. "Why are you calling Teresa? You just saw her a few hours ago. Why would you want to talk to her again so soon?"

"I don't have to give you a reason for calling a friend."

"You want her to get rid of me, don't you?"

Unlike Charley, Amanda could lie, but she saw no point in it. She leaned toward him, nose to ghostly nose. "Yes."

"It's not going to work. I won't leave you."

Amanda stormed into the kitchen, slammed open the refrigerator door, grabbed a Coke and yanked off the top then drank half of it.

He wasn't going to leave her and she couldn't leave him.

"Fine!" she shouted then realized he was, of course, right beside her. "Fine, but I'm going to live my life as if you aren't around. And if that includes doing things you don't like to see, well, you shouldn't be looking."

"I will be looking. Don't ever forget that."

She wasn't likely to forget.

᪣᪣

That afternoon while Amanda dressed for her date with Jake, Charley continued to make a nuisance of himself.

"Those jeans are way too tight. You should wear a pair of slacks, something that doesn't look so slutty."

"You need another button on that blouse. You could pin it so it doesn't go down so low."

"Makeup? You don't wear makeup very often, Amanda. I don't remember the last time you wore makeup for me. I guess this is a special night, huh? Getting all painted up to commit adultery."

"That lipstick is too red. You don't need lipstick that bright. You think this guy's gonna kiss it off you right in front of your husband?"

By the time she finished getting ready, she felt worn out and was beginning to question if the effort would be worth it. Charley was not going to let up. He would keep her a nervous wreck the entire evening. Maybe she should cancel. Surely Teresa would eventually figure out a way to help Charley progress to the next plane and then she could have a real date with Jake.

She picked up her cell phone. It seemed to weigh a ton, about the same as her heart at that moment. "All right. You win. I'm going to call Jake and cancel."

Charley smiled. "I'm glad you understand. It's the right thing to do."

245

Amanda checked her watch. Fifteen till six. He was probably on his way over already but he'd have his cell with him.

Someone knocked on the front door. Too late. For a moment she felt elation at the thought of seeing Jake. That flicker of elation was replaced immediately by a dark, leaden feeling. She'd have to send him away.

"Damn! Now you'll have to get rid of him in person." Charley vanished through the bedroom wall to the living room. Of course he'd go out to meet Jake and say rude things while she was trying to tactfully break their date without jeopardizing a future one.

With a sigh of resignation, she put her phone in her purse and started toward the door.

Charley appeared in front of her, blocking her path. "Don't answer that!"

"Get out of my way. Don't worry. I'll tell him I'm sick or something. It wouldn't be fair to subject him to an evening of you."

"It's not Jake. Don't answer it."

"Then who is it? It can't be Collins. He's in the hospital with two bullet holes." She went around him then through him as he again tried to block her.

"Amanda, please come back. Please don't answer that."

She opened the door to find Teresa standing there. Charley had tried to keep her from answering the door because he was afraid Teresa would send him to another plane. Good grief. She couldn't date and now she couldn't even have a friend?

"I'm sorry I'm so late," Teresa said. "I've had appointments all day, which is good because I need the money, but I know you need me too."

"Yeah, I do. Come on in, but it's a little late to try to get rid of Charley. Jake should be here any minute."

Teresa smiled as she moved inside, a big, happy smile. "I should have known Charley wouldn't tell you."

"Tell me what?"

Charley had vanished. That was strange. He must really be scared. Odd that he'd been worried about Teresa's welfare the night before and now he was avoiding her.

Teresa closed the door and looked around. "Charley, come here. We have to tell Amanda."

Charley came through the bedroom wall, straight to Teresa's side, moving as if someone was dragging him. He wasn't doing his usual pretense of walking. He kept his gaze on the floor and he didn't look happy.

"You should have told her." Teresa turned to Amanda. "Last night I had just got home and was pouring myself a glass of wine when Charley suddenly appeared."

"At your place? Charley came to your place without me? He was able to get that far away from me?" She looked at Charley. He continued to stare at the floor.

"Yes. He was as shocked as I was. He said he'd been thinking about me, concerned about me, and suddenly he found himself there with me."

"That's good. I'm glad he's expanding his area. But it still doesn't solve my problem. Even if he has the ability to go away and let me have some time without him, he won't."

Teresa's smile widened and her eyes sparkled. "There's one more thing. When I told him I was doing okay, he started to leave to return to you. I called him back because I wanted to try to persuade him to spend this evening with me and let you have your time with Jake. That's when we both discovered I can call him to me and he has to come."

Amanda's jaw dropped. She closed her mouth and looked at Charley. "Is that true?"

He didn't lift his gaze or answer her.

"He doesn't want to admit it," Teresa said, "but I assure you, it is true. Apparently last night when I was trying to work with him to help him progress, he and I became attached. I suspect it was because he was fighting me so hard. If you'd done the right thing and moved on, Charley, it wouldn't have happened."

Amanda smiled. "Does this mean what I think it means?"

"It does. I have nothing planned for the evening and will be happy to do a little ghost-sitting."

Amanda felt so light she thought she might be able to float the way Charley did. "Thank you! How can I ever repay you?"

"I've always wanted to learn to ride a motorcycle. Ross and I have a date tomorrow night, so you're on your own then, but I think we can work out a schedule."

She gave Teresa a hug. "I'm so glad you're my friend!"

"Come on, Charley. Let's go to my place and make popcorn. I'll send him home tomorrow, Amanda."

"Tomorrow?" Charley protested. "You want me to leave her alone all night?"

Teresa started down the steps with Charley trailing behind, grabbing at the rail, desperately and futilely attempting to halt his progress.

Jake, his foot on the bottom step, looked up. "Hi, Teresa."

"Hi, Jake. You and Amanda have a good time tonight."

Jake grinned. "We will."

"Wife stealer." Charley punched Jake in the nose as he and Teresa passed.

Jake blinked and looked surprised but then continued up the stairs to Amanda. "You look great. Beautiful."

"So do you. Look great, I mean. Maybe not beautiful. Handsome."

"I'm going to puke," Charley called. He sat stiffly in Teresa's car, in the passenger seat, not on the back.

Teresa waved and drove away, taking Charley with her.

Jake took Amanda's arm and smiled down at her. "Ready?"

She returned his smile. "Oh, yes. I am totally ready."

Ready to have a life that didn't always include Charley. Ready to see where this attraction with Jake could lead. Ready for a good-night kiss from warm, living lips.

The afternoon sun shone brightly on the horizon and in Amanda's heart as she walked down the steps with Jake.

THE END

About the Author:

I grew up in a small rural town in southeastern Oklahoma where our favorite entertainment on summer evenings was to sit outside under the stars and tell stories. When I went to bed at night, instead of a lullaby, I got a story. That could be due to the fact that everybody in my family has a singing voice like a bullfrog with laryngitis, but they sure could tell stories—ghost stories, funny stories, happy stories, scary stories.

For as long as I can remember I've been a storyteller. Thank goodness for computers so I can write down my stories. It's hard to make listeners sit still for the length of a book! Like my family's tales, my stories are funny, scary, dramatic, romantic, paranormal, magic.

Besides writing, my interests are reading, eating chocolate and riding my Harley.

Contact information is available on my website. I love to talk to readers! And writers. And riders. And computer programmers. Okay, I just plain love to talk!

http://www.sallyberneathy.com

70909239R00139

Made in the USA
Columbia, SC
24 August 2019